COMING FOR CHRISTMAS

SEXY ROMANTIC STANDALONE #1

KRYSTYNA ALLYN

To the ladies of B.A.N.G. book club,
I channeled my inner naughty girl to come up with this
doozy, and I hope you enjoy it.

WARNING:

This book contains FF, MM, MF, and MFM sexual content. If you have no idea what that means, then keep reading. You won't be disappointed.

CHAPTER 1

Woman Seeking Man, Seeking Man

BETHANY

"I CAN'T BELIEVE I'm doing this, Carrie," I declare to my best friend on the other line. I'm currently sitting in a coffee shop, listening to another annoying Christmas song, while waiting to meet with not just one, but two men.

"Well, honey, this is on your bucket list, so I guess it's okay. Though usually when you post Craigslist ads, murderers tend to answer. Are you sure they aren't planning your demise?"

"Yes, I'm sure. I vetted them before I even agreed to meet in person." And I definitely did. With a world full of crazies, you can't be too careful.

Prospect one's name is Cooper Whitmore. Divorced father of a three-year-old son, whose mother has primary custody. He works full time as an accountant, frequents baseball games, and might have a slight gambling problem. When I first saw he had a kid, I almost deleted his email, but his photo kept me interested, meaning, I felt a quiver in between my legs at his boy-next-door good looks. His blond hair is neatly trimmed, not a strand out of place. Those hazel eyes are a contradiction to his appearance. They shine with a glint of mischief and send a subliminal message that says I am going to destroy that pussy. How could I say no?

Selection number two is hot in a completely different way. Jared Carrington has this *Master of the Universe* air about him. He runs a hedge fund, and from my experience, those business types have alpha-male tendencies, along with major control issues. His photo was just as telling as Cooper's. His tailored appearance, expensive watch, and cufflinks tell me he likes the finer things in life. His assessing leaf-green eyes and inky cropped black hair add another dimension to his magnetism. He's single, but from what I've heard, he's fucked tons of the women at my office, so I have it on high authority that the man knows how to use his dick. The question is, can he handle me?

"Well, whatever you do, just make sure they wear condoms. Any men who agree to this probably have dirty dicks, and you don't want to catch herpes. You know that shit doesn't go away, right? I've seen pictures, and it's not pretty."

"Relax, Carrie." I sigh. "We've all been tested and cleared for this. Actually, I prefer no condoms to get the full experience."

"You make it sound like it's a ride in Disney World."

I grin into my coffee cup as I take a sip, setting it on the table afterward. "Well, it sort of is … a ride that is."

Carrie groans, and I chuckle.

"When are they supposed to arrive?"

"In a few, and before you ask, I've already emailed you my whereabouts and their information in case I disappear." I pull my phone away from my ear, take a quick selfie and then send it to her."

"Did you get the pic I just sent?"

"Yup, might I just say, you look extra slutty today."

Rolling my eyes I tell her, "You're just mad because you can't rock this look."

"Nah, I'm content not being a fire crotch ginger like you. And your White Walker looking pale blue eyes are creepy."

"Shut it." I giggle.

"Fine, fine. Go mentally prep for your Craigslist stalkers. Don't haunt me if they kill you and decide to use your skin for a body suit."

"No promises, babe. See ya."

I end the call before Carrie gets another word in. A pang of guilt hits me, because I told her a little white lie. She's under the impression that I posted my ad on Craigslist, but only a fool does that. Jared and Cooper's names were given to me through a kinky dating agency called *The Perfect Match.* My loose coworker, Danni, referred me to it.

Danni Sullivan is known as the office skank. No, she doesn't sleep her way to the top like others. All of her promotions are legit because she's smart and knows what she wants, from men, women, and occasionally both. Only the jealous women call her a skank, but to me, she's my hero. We go out drinking every week and each time, a different man picks her up. Once I asked her how she got so much play; she replied, "pussy power" and walked away with her Latin flavor that week.

One night, I was drunk and we got to talking about bucket lists. I mentioned that having a threesome was on the top of mine, but I had yet to find some guys as adventurous as me. I have no problem attracting men, but I always end up with the ones who can't even say boo. My last boyfriend, Mel, could barely get me to orgasm. He once told me that a man should always be gentle with his woman's lotus flower. Yes. The fucker called my pussy a lotus flower. I eventually dumped him because my vibrator got me to orgasm quicker than his dick.

After divulging to Danni my relationship fails and wants, she let me in on a secret dating company that matches people with others who have similar kinks. The fee was ridiculous, but I made a good amount of money as an executive assistant and managed to save a few bucks. I bought the three-month package, which included unlimited sexual encounters with your partner—or in my case, partners—a five-hundred-dollar gift certificate for toys, and four vouchers for hotel stays if the participants didn't have a suitable location for their sexual play. The company did an extensive background check to confirm I wasn't a narc. They sent me a series of photos with bios to choose from, and I narrowed it down to Cooper and Jared. Hopefully, I made the right choice.

The bell above the entrance to the coffee shop dings, indicating an arrival. I look up and see Cooper casually walk through the door. He brushes the snow from his coat and stomps his feet, removing the rest of the excess flakes. It's December 20th, and the weather gods decided to give New York a white Christmas. Since I live in Brooklyn, the snow is a pain in the ass because the city takes forever to plow the streets. Thank goodness only flurries are forecasted.

After Cooper orders a cup of coffee, he turns around and scans the crowd looking for me. Something about him seems familiar, but I can't quite place it. I give him a quick wave, and he plasters on an identical mischievous grin from his photos. He approaches the table, taking a seat across from me. Up close he's even hotter than I originally thought. His hair is unrulier than in his photo, but in a sexy way, the blond strands fall freely over his brow. He's sporting some light brown stubble on his chin, and the only thing I can think of at the moment is how it would feel between my legs.

Down girl, I mentally tell my pussy because she has been feenin ever since I made the decision to treat myself to this Christmas present.

"So …" Cooper starts, as I continue to think about my impending pleasure from this man.

"So," I reply, at a loss for words. What does one say to a man who will be participating in a threesome with you? Do you prefer anal or vaginal insertion? Should I even use the word insertion? Who even uses the word vaginal?

Shaking my head at my last thought, I extend my hand. "Hi, I'm Bethany Phillips, but you can call me Bee." He doesn't take my hand, which I find very rude, but I let him play his game.

"Bee?" he replies, raising an eyebrow at me. I actually hate my name, so I gave myself this nickname when I was ten, and refused to answer to Bethany or Beth. My parents were none too pleased with my declaration, but they eventually caved.

"Yes, Bee. I prefer it."

His lip twitches at my snarky tone. "Okay then, Bee. I'm Cooper, but you already know that."

Tilting his head to the side, he studies me, his perusal inquisitive, and not at all threatening. His gaze travels to the V in my white T-shirt and stops a beat too long. I'm guessing he's a breast man by the way he's licking his lips. Perfect, because I have nice tits. Even at the ripe old age of thirty, they're still as perky as they were when I was twenty-one.

"Eyes up here, Cooper," I snap, hiding the fact that I like him ogling my boobs.

"Sorry, I was only checking out the merchandise, and might I say, Daddy like."

Daddy?

"Err ... please don't ever use that word when we fuck. I have a father and don't want to picture him during sex."

"Sure thing. I'll *bee* good."

Rolling my eyes, I fold my arms across my chest. "Did you seriously just reference 'E.T.'?"

"Yes, I did." He grins. "Or would you prefer Bumblebee? They were both great movies."

"How about we stick to Bee, m'kay."

Laughing, Cooper holds his hands up in retreat. "I

like you, Bee. You make me laugh, and I suspect that you're a wild one in bed. I'm looking forward to getting you naked."

"Me too," I agree, blushing. I move the conversation along asking him, "So, why did you decide to join this service? After reading your file, you don't seem like the type who might be interested."

"I could say the same about you. Though with your red locks, you definitely have a freaky side."

"I'm not—"

"I believe your ad said, and I quote, 'I want to be fucked rough and dirty until my pussy weeps from too much pleasure.' Did I get that right?"

Covering my face with my hands I mutter, "Maybe." I was so excited to find a dating company that I may have went a bit overboard with my request.

"Don't worry about it, Bee. I'll give you anything you want because I might want the same too. As to why I joined the dating agency, I blame my ex-wife." Running a hand through his hair, Cooper goes into his story.

"Years of boring sex with that evil woman neutered me. I met her in college, and we used to do all the sinful things I wanted, but as soon as she said I do, it all changed. There no more morning closet quickies, or dirty bar bathroom fucks, because we felt like it. They were replaced with weekly trips to Home Depot and monthly arguments in Ikea. By the time my son was two, we had sex once every six months. It was pathetic. I got to a point where I was trolling for a prostitute. I never went through with the transaction, but that's when I knew I needed more. Of course, I approached my ex with these issues, but nothing changed. I divorced her and joined the dating service. My friend put in a good word for me. Best money I've ever spent."

"Hmm," was all I could say. I totally understood his feeling of unfulfillment. I've been like that since forever.

"All you have to say is 'hmm'? I thought I'd at least get some sympathy or an offer of a boob squeeze."

"You know, Cooper," I prop my elbow on the table and lean my chin into my hand, "I barely know you, yet you're being pretty open with me. Why is that?"

Shrugging, he responds, "I'm an open guy, and I figure since we're going to be naked together at some point, it would be best to get you in a relaxed state."

I like his answer. I'm not nervous about the sex per se. I've had plenty of no strings attached hookups, so I can handle the emotional baggage that comes with it.

"I should tell you I'm not looking for a boyfriend," I blurt out.

"You are just full of surprises." He laughs at my declaration. "No need to worry about me wanting a relationship. I'm still trying to exorcise my bitch ex-wife from my system. I'm all for the fun. Now about that boob squeeze ..."

"Are you ever serious?" I chuckle.

"Only when I'm naked. I like to concentrate on what I'm doing, and," his face comes close to mine, "I'm really good."

My breath hitches at his forwardness. He might be the boy next door, but somewhere deep inside, has little bit of devil in him. I want to kiss his full lips and almost do until the bell above the coffee shop door rings again. I look over Cooper's shoulder, and in walks Jared. Cooper turns his head and gives the man a chin lift as if they know each other. Then he leans back in the chair and smiles at me.

I watch Jared stalk like a predator to the barista and order a coffee. She is obviously taken by him based on her blush and the tremble of her hand when she hands him the coffee. The knowing smirk he gives the woman at the register tells me he realizes the effect he has on women, and the cocky fucker doesn't even care.

When Jared's eyes finally land on mine, chills travel through me, and though the room is warm, my body still shivers. This dark haired man has this powerful aura about him that demands attention and fuck if he doesn't have it from everyone in the room.

"You can close your mouth now," Cooper tells me as he uses his index finger to push my lips together.

Shit, I didn't even know it was open. As soon as I take in a deep breath, the enticing scent of Jared's cologne hits me, turning my mind to putty. No man should have this effect on anyone, especially looking like that.

Jared takes the seat next to Cooper and they greet each other. I feel like a voyeur watching their interaction, and I can tell that they are definitely close. How in the fuck did I manage to pick two men who have a personal relationship?

"How's it going, Jared? Still making elderly people bankrupt?"

"Fuck you, Coop," Jared replies smiling. "You still embezzling money?"

Jared turns to face me, and I visibly gulp. I'm fairly certain I look like Roger Rabbit with my cartoonishly —if that's a word—long tongue hanging out. He's giving me the same grin that he used on the woman at the counter, and it damn near expire in the spot.

"Yup," Cooper agrees. "How the hell else would I afford such a lovely dating package."

"So what do we have here?" The rumble in Jared's voice is so powerful that if I were standing, it would bring me to my knees. Another side effect of his sexy tone is the intensifying ache between my legs. Fucking hell this man is going to ruin me.

"This is Bee, Jared," Cooper answers for me, mirth in his gaze. "She has a fetish for being stung by bees. Something about being poked."

Regaining my faculties from all that is Jared, I shake my head at Cooper, giving him an exasperated look. "You're going to be a handful, aren't you?"

"Maybe."

I let out a sigh and turn to Jared, introducing myself. The suave bastard takes my hand, runs his nose along my knuckles, and places a soft kiss in the center.

"Thanks," I squeak, yanking my hand away. I could flirt with this man for the entire evening, but I should get to know him better before specifics are laid out.

"So, Jared, tell me a little more about yourself. Cooper here," I motion to the silent man, "gave me some background information."

"You have my file." I narrow my eyes at his clipped response. I already know what the file says, but I want more.

He smirks. "All you need to know is that I'm an expert at fucking, how did she describe it, Coop?"

"Rough and dirty," Cooper replies, grinning.

"Yes, that's it," Jared agrees. "No need for all this chitchat. Let's schedule a time to do this. I have a busy calendar and can fit you in ..." Jared pulls out his phone and scrolls. "Christmas Eve?"

"Same," Cooper concurs, after pulling out his phone too and reviewing his calendar.

This seems too easy, but throwing caution to the

wind, I agree with their date. As they both prepare to leave, I tell them to wait.

"I'm not finished yet, gentlemen. I have a few requirements for our play that I didn't mention in the email correspondence. I figured it's best to tell you up front because it's detailed." I smile sweetly at them as they both give me looks of interest.

"I'm up for anything," Cooper responds first as he spins his phone on the table.

"Sure," Jared tells me, though there is a slight narrowing of his eyes.

I let out a deep breath and explain my fantasy in detail to my captive audience. "When I was thirteen I found a porn tape in a box in my parents' basement. It was labeled music video, so of course, I wanted to see what the video was. As soon as I hit play, I realized that the only music in the video was the melody of moans and grunts of the three people fucking."

"Great," Cooper interrupts me. "You saw an old VHS style porn, where the men had fewer abs, and the women wore their lady bushes proudly." Jared chuckles and pats Cooper on the back as if his quip was a job well done.

"Shut it," I snap. "Let me finish."

"Go on, ginger," Cooper mocks. I know he's trying to be funny, but I still scowl at him.

"As I was saying, these three were really going at it, and it was so damn hot. I didn't know it at the time, but that experience changed how I viewed sex. I was so addicted to porn back then, that I would pay the town drunk to buy tapes for me from the adult store. I learned about how to pleasure myself and others, but was always afraid to take that extra step with my partner."

"Jeez," Jared mutters. "Sounds like we are exactly what you need." Hell yes, they are.

"So basically what I'm saying is that I've had time to plan out what I want and how I want it done." Reaching into my pocket, I pull out two separate pieces of paper and hand them to the men.

"What's this?" Cooper asks as he unfolds his paper.

"My requirements," I respond.

"Oh, this is going to be easy." He smiles at me.

Jared opens his paper next and gives me the look of death. "Seriously? You want this?"

I nod. "Yup. Do you think you can handle it?" He stares at the page for a beat too long. "Because I can ask someone else to take care of it."

"Fine," Jared grumbles, shoving the list in his pocket.

"Awesome. Follow the list exactly, and we'll all catch up when you get to number three."

"Wait, I didn't get to see what you gave him." Cooper laughs and attempts to go into Jared's pocket.

"Fuck off, Coop," Jared grumbles. "I'll take care of it, Bee, on one condition."

"Condition?" I sit up straight and prepare for an argument.

"Relax, I only want to call you Beth or Bethany, because this Bee shit doesn't work for me."

Oh, the alpha is coming out again.

I bite my bottom lip in contemplation. I guess with role-playing it's better that I let this name thing slide. "Fine."

"Thank fuck," Cooper shouts. "This will prevent my mind from drifting to E.T. as I drill you. You saved my life, Jared. I owe you one."

"Didn't I just tell you to fuck off?"

"Yes, you did, but you know that I don't scare easily."

"Okay, guys, you have your assignments," I interrupt their bromance weirdness, "but at some point, you two are going to tell me how you know each other. I'm letting it slide for now because I want to get ready for our night."

They both give me the same sly grin, stand, and leave the coffee shop. After their departure, I lean back in my chair and take a deep breath. I'm so going to do this, and if these two men are as good as I think they will be, this shit is going to be epic.

CHAPTER 2

Location, Location

COOPER

"IF YOU'RE NOT HERE by eleven, Coop, then forget about the afternoon with him."

"Are you serious right now?" I grip my phone tight as I stand outside the hotel I'm scoping out. It's Monday morning, the day after our first in-person meeting and Beth asked me to find a swanky hotel. She gave me certain parameters for the place she wanted us to do the deed, and I don't want to fuck this up. Unfortunately, I have to deal with my ex first.

"The court said that I can deny a visit if you don't come on time, and that's what I'm doing," she shouts through the phone. I momentarily pull it away from my ear because it's so damn loud.

"You know that's bullshit, Britt. I'll be there on time, I'm running an errand first."

"I know all about your errands," she spits. "You should really change your address with the bank. I saw a large payment to a *The Perfect Match* dating service on one of your statements. Is that where you find your whores now?"

Groaning, I rub my hand down my face. "That's none of your damn business. We. Are. Divorced. What I choose to do with my dick and money on my free time has nothing to do with you or my son." I'm pacing back and forth because this woman makes me crazy.

"Maybe I should show this to the court since you seem to care more about who you fuck rather than your son."

Through clenched teeth, I tell her, "I'll be there on time."

"Okay. We need to talk." Shit, her voice goes from harsh to sweet in a matter of moments. Who knows what the hell she wants this time.

"Whatever," I mutter, ending the call before she has a chance to poison me with more of her words.

My ex-wife is such a fucking cunt.

Yes.

A cunt.

I used to think that word should never apply to any female, but after my sham of a marriage to that woman, I changed my tune completely. The only good thing that came out of our relationship was our wonderful son Alex.

I met Brittany Amber Wilson in college and stupidly thought it was love at first sight. I was dead wrong. She was and still is a master manipulator. When I think back to the first time I saw her brown eyes, ran my fingers through her thick dark hair, and palmed that curvy ass of hers, I can see how I was blinded.

My dick knew what it wanted, and my brain went along with it. I would have never met her if I weren't hungover from the night before and ended up in the wrong classroom at the wrong time. When the teacher came in and announced that I was in African American History, I hurriedly packed my bag and prepared to leave. Don't get me wrong; I would have taken the class if I didn't have so many electives that semester. I think it's important to learn about other cultures and what better place than in a college melting pot.

After the last book was thrown in my bag, this beauty sat next to me, and I had to know her. The smoothness of her light brown skin was like a vision, and I almost reached out and touched her face the first time. Of course, I stopped myself because she probably would have punched me. What I did do was sit through the entire class, and the next one, until the professor realized that I didn't belong. Eventually, I got her number and the rest was history.

I like fucking ... a lot, and she satisfied me the entire time we dated. I thought we'd go on like that for a while until she proved me wrong months after the wedding. I don't know if it was her friends' influences or the fact that she was always a bitch that caused our downfall. She would withhold sex to get me to do things for her, mainly spend money. I made a decent living, but I also had a trust fund from my grandparents, which I didn't plan on touching. But then Brittany would need a new pair of shoes, or maybe a better car, or weekly hair and nail appointments. I appreciated the fact that she wanted to keep herself beautiful for me, but it got to be too much. Coupled with the fact that I was horny all the time. I attempted to make it work, but the prostitution incident told me that she was toxic to my psyche. I needed to escape. I didn't get arrested, thank goodness. It made me realize that I never wanted another woman to hold that much power over me again.

The hustle and bustle of Times Square brings me back to the present, and I stare at the hotel of my choice, the InterContinental. I researched several other New York City luxury hotels. However, the layout of this place fits what Beth described. I couldn't choose between the Manhattan Bay Suite and the Penthouse, so I thought it prudent to come in person, deciding then.

A burst of excitement hits me as I stare up at the lavish building. The outside structure is a mix of old and new, with the brown and tan bricks on the lower floors and the steely skyscraper built on top, a true Manhattan hotel.

The doorman smiles as he grabs the gold colored handle of the tall glass doors and motions for me to enter. My senses are assailed with the sounds of clicking shoes across the black marble floor, the squeaky wheels of the luggage carts, and the incessant chatter from the clerks at the registration desk. The soothing scent of pine from the Christmas tree located in the center of the lobby permeates throughout the room, its exquisitely designed ornaments a testament to the high-end locale.

Striding around one of the tall brown pillars, I head directly to the concierge and wait for the man to finish his call. The tone of his voice is highbrow, and by that I mean snooty. In my business, I've dealt with this type before, people pleasers. They're great when you need something, but annoying when you don't.

When he stands to greet me, having finished his call, his features become more evident. He has a slender, less than masculine figure and a platinum-blond ponytail that extenuates the angular structure of his face. Add the expensive looking suit, and you have yourself an example of a project runway contestant. I may or may not have watched that show once or twice with the ex.

"Welcome to the InterContinental, sir." His eyes scan my body a little too long, and when I give him a gotcha look, a blush forms on his cheeks. I'm not wearing anything special, a simple charcoal gray suit with a black collared shirt. No tie because it's my day off.

Extending my hand, I introduce myself to the man who is showing an interest other than professional to me. I have this effect on both sexes. "Hi. I'm Cooper Whitmore. I have a nine forty-five with Ms. Brooks." He takes my hand in greeting.

"I'm Bradley, her assistant. Unfortunately, she is out sick today, but I can take you on the tour you requested."

"No problem," I reply. The poor guy hasn't let go yet, but I won't call him on it. I merely tug my hand back gently, not enough to startle him. Clearing his throat, Bradley directs me to the elevators. As we enter, Bradley drones on about the history of the hotel and the renovations. I zone out the entire time, occasionally throwing in a mm-hmm or wow, in order to pretend I'm interested. My thoughts go to Beth instead.

The minute I saw that ginger, I was hooked. She is the perfect mixture of innocence, with a side of devilish behavior, and I can't wait to get her naked. I thank my lucky stars that she picked me and Jared. I've known him for years, and we have shared women before, so what she asks for is no big deal. I don't foresee this turning into a relationship, but I am definitely open to anything when it comes to her. Jared couldn't care less. He is a sexual being as much as I am, but he prefers variety.

"And here we are." The dinging of the elevator on the 33rd floor pulls me back to the present. I follow Bradley down a short hallway, and moments later he opens the door to the massive suite.

"This is the Manhattan Bay Suite," he tells me, motioning toward the tall glass windows. "There are two full bathrooms, including a rain shower and a soaking bathtub." Flashes of fucking Beth in the shower run through my mind as Bradley mentions something about square footage and dining room seating.

"The nightly rate is two thousand, and we would need a credit card payment for one night to hold it."

"Sure I'll take it, but I need a favor."

Bradley raises an eyebrow at me, and before he has a chance to ask me what the request is, I divulge, "I'm going to be honest with you, Brad. Can I call you Brad?"

"Uh, sure, Mr. Whitmore, but I'd have to ask my manager if you need ..."

"Let's not get any managers involved. Can we keep this between you and me?" I grin and throw on some smolder to get his interest, his blush a clear indicator that I have him for the most part.

"I need this place for two nights, but I have to make certain changes. I realize that it's against hotel policy to do anything that would alter the room. However, I'm willing to do whatever you like if you agree to keep my secret."

"I-I can't lose my job, Mr. Whitmore, I'm—"

"Shh, Brad." I put a hand on his shoulder, squeezing it gently, being sure to add a little thumb rubbing action at the end. The man shivers, and I nearly laugh. By no means am I into guys, but I'm not afraid to use my natural God-given talents to get what I want.

"What exactly do you need?" he questions me, as I let go and give him one of my sexy grins.

"Well, Brad, I plan on having an ... interesting weekend with a woman, and a man." His eyes widen as I smile. "And the changes that I have to make involve certain extracurricular *appliances* if you will." Actually, I need to drill a hole in the wall for a sex swing, but I don't tell him that. "I'm asking that you keep the staff away from my room Saturday night. I know that you guys keep a tight ship here and you want to make sure that high-end guests are taken care of, however, we won't need any help at all."

Crossing my arms in front of my chest, I wait for Brad's response. I can tell that he's thinking hard about it by the way he bites his bottom lip.

"Okay," he agrees, "but umm can I watch?" Brad whispers, and I can barely hide the shock on my face. Maybe I should give him the name of the dating agency. No, I have an even better idea.

"Sorry, Brad, but my other partners aren't into that. How about I give you something for your spank bank I know you'll enjoy." I can't believe I'm about to do this, but getting into Beth's pants is my top priority. With the limited time I have to secure a location, I'll do whatever I have to in order to make this happen.

Walking up the stairs to the bathroom I begin to undress. I check behind me to see if Brad is following, and yup, he so is. At this point, I'm down to my black silk boxers, and the chill of the air conditioner is giving me goose bumps. I turn on the shower, looking forward to the steamy warmth the water will bring.

"Have a seat on the toilet and watch me. The number one rule, Brad, is no touching me. If you'd like to touch yourself, then, by all means, go for it."

As soon as I drop my boxers, I hear an audible gasp come from the young man. I'm already hard, and not because of him. I use the vision of Beth's tits as a focal point and little Coop comes to attention.

The heat of the water hits my skin and I moan at the contact. I'm not acting out for the purpose of Brad and whatever his dirty thoughts are, the water feels that fucking good. Grabbing the soap, I rub it slowly across my chest, creating an ample amount of suds. I want this to last more than a couple of minutes, so I move on to my hair, running my hands through it like a porn star. When I do the proverbial shake of my head, I hear the echo of a belt being unbuckled and this is when I realize that shit just got real.

Lathering up my hands again, I glide one of them down my abs, eventually gripping myself at the base of my cock. I'm still hard because Beth does that to me.

First, I picture her tits peeking out at me at the coffee shop … stroke, stroke. Beth jogging, her tight ass in the gray exercise pants … stroke, stroke. Her, in a Tigers cheerleader outfit … stroke, stroke. The speed of my glide increases tenfold, and I groan when my hips thrust faster into my fist. Rubbing myself off feels so fucking phenomenal that I don't even hear the heavy breathing and eventual coming of Brad.

"Fuck," I growl as I come all over my hand, spilling on the shower floor. I've never done anything like this before, but it actually wasn't that bad. I chance a glance at Brad and see that his pants are at his ankles, his face is red, and hand covered in his own release.

"We got a deal, Brad?" I give him another smile. He stares at me wide-eyed, but nods. "Good. Give me a few minutes to clean up, and we'll talk more about the fees."

"S-sure," he stutters as he cleans himself up and leaves. I can barely contain my glee at my success, and I can't wait to tell Beth. It will have to wait though because I need to deal with my bitch of an ex-wife. This weekend can't get here fast enough.

CHAPTER 3

Boys And Their Toys

JARED

Coop: Hotel is a go.

I ROLL my eyes at Cooper's text because I know that I need to come through with my part next. I've never been ordered by someone, let alone a woman, to do any task that doesn't involve fucking her hard, until now. I'm usually the boss, master of the fucking universe, and have been since I got my first promotion at the ripe old age of twenty-two. I know what I want, how to get it, and usually, do, but right now as I stare at the outside of The Pleasure Chest sex shop, I'm so out of my element.

In no way am I a prude; I've just never had the urge to use a sex toy. My huge dick is the epitome of a toy, and I have several satisfied conquests that will attest to that fact. Shit, I could provide Beth with references if she asked. Unfortunately, the woman wants what she wants, and I'm inclined to give it to her, for Cooper's sake. That's what good friends do for each other.

As soon as I enter the mostly empty store, a barrage of Fa La La La La's hits me like a knife in the gut. It's not that I dislike Christmas. It's the music that makes me want to vomit. I don't understand how people consciously listen to this rubbish as early as Thanksgiving. I've actually thrown rocks at carolers before. In my defense, it was college, and I was drunk.

Before I have a musical mental breakdown, I'm greeted by a sales associate with a name tag that reads Nikki. She's pretty, but as I glance around the room, I notice that all of the women are beautiful. I'm wondering if it's some ploy to get men to buy more of this shit by picturing their clerks using it. My eyes go back to Nikki, with her enticing curly dirty blond shoulder-length locks and that slim waist and all I can think is, damn. Then the woman licks her lips like she's preparing to eat me for lunch, and I know I'm in trouble.

"Can I help you with ... something?" she asks me in a breathy tone I'm all too familiar with. Most women react the same way when they meet me, and I can get them in bed anytime I want. If I didn't have plans with Beth, I'd consider this Nikki woman. Her plump red lips would look so good wrapped around my cock. I even have a flash of me gripping that wild blond mane of hers while I thrust into her mouth.

Shit. My dick just came to attention.

Clearing my throat, I tell her, "I have a list of things that I need for a umm ... friend." She arches an eyebrow at me.

"A friend?"

"Yes," I respond as I pull the piece of paper out of my pocket.

Nikki walks the short distance to me and whispers in my ear, "I'd like to be your friend."

Inwardly, I groan at her closeness. She doesn't realize that if she takes another step forward, she will come in contact with my aching erection.

"I always need more friends," I mention casually, subliminally sending her my dirty thoughts. Then, reaching into my other pocket, I grab my business card. She takes it and grins. No sense in losing out on guaranteed free pussy. "But for today, I need some things for my other friend. Be sure to reach out to me in a week so that we can become closer … friends."

She nods and then goes back to what must be her business mode.

"Mr.?" I just realized I didn't even tell her my name. "Carrington, Jared Carrington. You can call me Jared."

Blushing, she extends her hand and responds, "Nice to meet you, Jared, now what can I get for you?"

Going to the paper in my hand, I read the first thing on the list. "What can you tell me about sex swings?" Her eyes widen and the blush on her face deepens. She obviously thinks she's hit the jackpot with me, and she has, though I don't use extras.

"I have an idea, Jared. Let me take you to the back room for a personal display of all that we have to offer. I like to fully satisfy my customers."

Hell yes. "I inwardly rejoice, though part of me knows this is a bad idea.

Turning on her heels, she directs me to a back door. I am so entranced by her ass that I didn't see the other store clerk follow. I whirl to face the other woman as soon as I hear the click of the lock behind me. Her name tag reads Shannon but my eyes don't go to her face. She has the biggest tits I've ever seen in my life, and her tiny waist accentuates the fullness of her boobs. And that blond hair, similar to Nikki's, they could pass for twins in the right lighting. Fuck me, I can't be awake. Two women, a back room, and a sex shop are a recipe for something hot and dirty. I swear that I've had this dream before.

No, I tell myself. I'm not allowed to screw anyone until after my Beth and Cooper adventure. The STD tests have been taken, and Beth's proof of birth control given. She wants this whole experience bare. Condom or not, I can't fuck this up for Coop. I owe the guy my life.

"So you want a sex swing?" Nikki asks in a sultry tone. "Do you have any idea what kind?"

"Uh," I stutter as I take a seat on the chaise against the wall. "What kinds are there?"

"Well, sweetie," Shannon interjects, "depends on where you want it mounted. I prefer freestanding because it holds your partner's weight better, but there are door, wall, and ceiling mounted versions. Why don't you tell me exactly how you plan to use it, and me and Nikki will give you a small demonstration." Shannon gives me a grin filled with desire.

Fuck it, I decide to be honest because, let's face it, this whole scenario is hot. "I'm participating in a threesome with a woman and another man." I give them both a toothy grin. "I think the ceiling mounted swing sounds good," I tell them in a gravelly tone, barely able to contain my lust for this situation. "Can you show me your best one?"

"We definitely can do that." As they both disappear

into another hidden room, I shoot Cooper a quick text.

Me: You motherfucker.

Coop: Christmas shopping with Alex. What the fuck did I do now?

I hate bothering him when he's with his son. His bitch of an ex makes life hard for him, but I need to get this shit off my chest.

Me: At a sex shop with the opportunity to fuck two women.

Coop: You better keep that shit in your pants.

Me: I realize that ...

Coop: Good.

Me: I just wanted to inform you that you owe me big for this.

Coop: Yeah, yeah ... you owe me so much more. <eye roll>

Me: I will not screw these women, but I will have some fun.

Coop: Keep your dick stowed, dude. I don't want Beth or me to catch anything.

Me: No promises about the stowing, but I will keep it to myself.

Coop: Okay enough dick talk with you. This is a weird conversation.

Me: You brought it up.

Coop: Fuck off.

Coop: Buy 2 cock rings ... blame Beth for that one.

Me: <Groan> Fuck, fine.

The women enter the room again as I shove my phone back into my pocket. Shit, shit, they're wearing the same lingerie, red lace bra with matching panties, a fucking garter belt with stockings, and red heels. Keep it together, I tell myself. However, I'm a man and I have needs.

Shaking off my sexual hunger for the moment, I

notice that they are carrying a series of straps, hooks, and padding. I watch quietly as Nikki stands on a chair and attaches one part to the ceiling while Shannon adjusts the other parts. It looks rather complicated, but I'm no dummy and can figure it out. There's also YouTube.

The bulging erection causes my pants to tighten as Nikki begins to fasten Shannon in the swing, the noise of the Velcro making my throat dry. What I wouldn't give to have my mouth in between Shannon's legs to taste her. Fuck. This stowing of my dick is harder than I thought. I haven't had many temptations since I agreed to do this, but my resolve is slowly disappearing. Nikki turns to face me while Shannon lies back in the swing comfortably as if she does this on a daily basis.

"This is what's called The Screamer Twist Sex Swing," Nikki explains. "Screamer is definitely top of the line when it comes to swings, but this new one adds an extra layer of kink because …" She goes to Shannon, whose back is to her. "It spins. And I'm thinking that with your upcoming activities you might want something this versatile." She uses a hand and twirls the swing around. My cock goes completely rigid when Nikki informs me, "Let me show you one of the positions that works well with the swing."

Leaning forward, I avidly watch as Nikki slowly drags Shannon's panties down and spreads her legs.

Holy hell, the girl is bare down there. I loosen the tie from around my neck because I'm sweating like a motherfucker. I've been with two women before, but never in this way. I might have to give sex toys a try after this experience. My breath hitches as soon as Nikki circles her tongue on Shannon's clit, causing her coworker to moan. This goes on for what feels like forever, and I eventually break down, deciding to stroke myself. I figure that as long as I don't touch them, I should be fine.

Unbuckling my belt, I pull out my dick and begin to glide my hand up and down my shaft. Shannon turns her head my way, her wanton gaze leisurely trails down my chest, pausing at my cock. I smirk because she realizes how big I am. Licking her lips, she pulls out those enormous tits and pinches her nipples. I groan in response.

Nikki is really into Shannon's pussy because the girl hasn't come up for air yet. The sex god in me feels bad. Everyone deserves pleasure, and I have to give a little to Nikki for her show.

"I also need vibrators," I add, the sexual promise in my words evident.

"I figured as much," Nikki tells me after raising her head from a panting Shannon. She glides her tongue across her top lip when she discovers me still stroking myself.

"I have two that you can," she pauses, biting her lip,

"test out." I follow Nikki with my eyes as she steps away from Shannon and goes to a bag on the floor pulling out two separate boxes. She gets both devices out in record time and sets them on the table to the right of where Shannon still swings.

"This is what's called a Womanizer Deluxe." I stare at the vibrator, and at first glance, there doesn't appear to be anything special about it. The oval shape and floral design mean nothing to me unless it gets Beth off. "It can get a woman off in two minutes or less." Fuck. My eyes widen. "It's called pleasure air technology. This thing mimics the act of oral sex without all of the touching." She points to a circular part on the other side of the vibrator that looks unassuming. "But before I get to that, here's another one that works just as well if not better."

This woman is trying to kill me because when she shows me the next thing, I nearly expire on the spot.

"I own The Fifty Shades of Grey Greedy Girl, and it was the best purchase I ever made. This gem has simultaneous G-spot and clitoral stimulation thanks to the dual motors. I've had multiple orgasms alone and with a partner." Nikki winks at me. "Oh, and if you're interested in a little anal play, I have a Love Honey glass butt plug that goes in easy and doesn't require that much lubrication. Which would you like me to show you first?"

I'm officially out of control. The entire time that

Nikki explained the ins and outs of these toys, I was giving myself quick and steady strokes. This has to be one of the hottest moments of my life, and there is no fucking way that I'm denying myself some sort of release.

"Show me all of them," I growl as I stalk toward her. She gives me a sensual smirk and then turns to Shannon. I pause mid-stride and watch as she rubs the glass plug all over Shannon's pussy, eventually dragging it to her tight crevice and sliding it in.

"That's one," Nikki breathes as she runs her tongue along Shannon's clit again. I grip the base of my cock hard, to prevent myself from coming. That shit was hot as fuck, and I almost blew my load. The obviously sexually adventurous girl then takes the Womanizer, uses her fingers to spread Shannon's pussy apart, and places the suction on her clit. She turns it on the lowest setting, but it appears as though it doesn't matter. Shannon is rocking her hips on the swing like she's being fucked hard. Dammit all to hell, I want her to be sucking my dick right now.

"That's two," Nikki whispers in my ear, bringing my attention back to her. I reach out my hand in an attempt to grab the Fifty fucker, but she shakes her head no.

"This isn't an interactive show." My mouth drops as she casually walks by me and lies down on the chaise I just walked away from. "You can ... watch. Perhaps get some pointers for your friend." I nod because what the hell else could I do.

Nikki begins to fuck herself with the Grey thing and her moans are driving me crazy. Coupled with the fact that Shannon is writhing uncontrollably from her anal and clitoral stimulations on the swing. This whole scene is insane, arousing, and goddamn magnificent. I loosen my pants completely and the belt makes a clinking sound when it hits the floor. I'm unsure who I want to focus on, Nikki on my right with those fuckable lips or Shannon on my left with her great tits. I decide it's prudent to stand in the center and jack myself off. The faster I go, the more shallow my breath. I've never wanted to come so bad in my life, and this one will be a doozy.

"Tell me how big my dick is," I order, my gaze going to Shannon first.

"It's so big," she breathes as she squeezes her tits and thrusts her hips into the air. "I can't wait for you to be inside of me."

"Fuck, that's right, baby. You want this dick, too, don't you, Nikki?" My cock is as hard as stone, and I'm so close, so fucking close to release.

"Yes," she shouts, the sounds of her pleasure becoming louder with each thrust of the vibrator. "I need your big dick in my mouth, in my pussy, in my ass … everywhere."

Shannon finishes first, and the noises that come

from deep within her are guttural like she's exorcised a sex-obsessed demon. Nikki goes next, her climax equally as primal. Now, it's my turn, and fuck, do I come.

Multiple ropes of semen shoot from my dick in successive waves hitting the floor. The feeling of a satisfying release is never-ending, and at one point, I think I will keel over and die.

"So damn good," I groan, satisfied. "I'll take everything, and add two of your favorite cock rings."

An alarm goes off and both girls mutter the word "shit" at the same time. Nikki rushes over to Shannon, removing all of the toys and unhooking her from the swing. I barely have a chance to pull my pants up, when they shoo me out of the back room. The one clerk in the waiting area gives me a knowing smirk, and I shrug and smile back.

As I wait for my purchases, the main door opens and the store becomes inundated with people. The lonely clerk rolls her eyes before approaching a customer. I'm wondering why she's so annoyed, but then I realize the reason for the sudden crowd.

"I want to buy the same sex toy as Samantha," a woman with a thick southern accent shouts to a man standing in the corner. "Becky said I was a Samantha, so I need it."

"Fine dear," the man mutters. His clothing is GQ tourist central with the Hawaiian shirt and dad jeans. I suddenly feel the need to escape, because I know what's coming next.

"Hey," a woman startles me from behind. "Are you Mr. Big?"

"No," I snap, walking away from the loon to wait at the register. "Of course you are. The dark hair, the suit. Can I be your Carrie?"

"Listen, lady, I don't know who Mr. Big and Carrie are, but if you don't back the fuck up, I'll have you arrested." I actually do know, but I have to keep the crazies away. It's best to play dumb.

She sighs. "Such a Big response." I roll my eyes and ignore her.

"Hey Carnie, Wynonna, Sue Ellen," she shouts. "I found Mr. Big. Come see."

Motherfucker. I would end up at this sex shop.

Shannon and Nikki show up at the register just in time and ring me up. I hand them my credit card and quickly finish the transaction.

"Have those delivered to the address on the card, and ladies," they both look at me grinning, "I have some time next week for more demonstrations. Bring everything that you'll need."

Both nodding, I wave at them and depart the store before the *Sex and the City* brigade accost me again. With this done, I move on to the next part of Beth's plan of preparation.

CHAPTER 4

Manscaping And Other Things

BETHANY

"ARE you sure I need to do this?" Cooper whispers low in my ear as we sit in the waiting area of Dana's Spa & Salon on the Upper East Side of Manhattan.

"Yes," I hiss, rubbing my eyes. One of my requirements was that everyone is hairless. With everything that we'll be doing, who wants a mouthful of fur? Not me.

This place is uber fancy, with its glass shelving, wooden floors, and Brooks Brothers massage chairs in the waiting room. I chose this location because it was in the vicinity of our offices.

When we first walked into the salon, Cooper mentioned getting his face shaved. However, when I explained to him exactly what hair was being removed, he paled. Jared couldn't give two shits because he gets his body taken care of on a regular basis. I only found this out because the receptionist greeted him by name and asked if he wanted the usual.

"Seriously, Beth, I think it's perfectly normal for a man to have hair wherever." He grips my forearm and stares at me with a panicky expression. "What if they pull my skin off? I've seen that happen in movies, and it looks painful."

Placing a comforting arm on his shoulder, I inform him, "They have different wax for those sensitive areas." He shivers and I damn near chuckle.

"I'm blaming you if my dick falls off," Cooper complains.

"Calm down, man." Jared strolls in from the back room in a robe and flip-flops, looking relaxed. *Is he wearing sexy elf boxers?* "The ladies in the back are careful with your manhood, and they do a good job."

"Mr. Jared," a petite Asian woman shuffles from the back, "you forgot this." She hands him a glass of champagne and then bows.

"Thank you, Suki." He reaches out, grabs the glass,

and swallows the contents. "Throw an extra five percent tip on my bill. Same time next week?"

"Yes, Mr. Jared." She bows again and backs out of the room.

Cooper gives Jared an are-you-fucking-serious look, while Jared returns a smug smile.

"Been going here for years." He shrugs. When you get as much sex as I do, you have to keep your shit maintained."

Cooper opens his mouth to say something but is interrupted when the masseuse calls his name.

"Oh shit," I mutter as I take in the person assigned to wax Cooper.

He immediately goes bug-eyed when the brawny woman with a unibrow walks toward him. Her bulky arms rival that of The Rock, and that mustache is so thick that it should have its own area code. Cooper's face is so comical that I can barely keep it together, and Jared is leaning against the counter cracking up as well.

"No," Cooper shouts like a petulant child. "I will not let Shrek go anywhere near my junk. She has man-beast hands that could break me. I want Suki."

"Calm down, Coop," Jared says while still laughing. "Helga here is the best at waxing. She's in high demand."

"You lying fucker," Cooper growls as he stands and begins pacing the room.

He looks at me pleading, and I must admit that his pouty face is cute. I almost cave because of it.

"Go with Helga," I coax him. "I can come in and hold your hand if you like." He glares at me, but I return with a grin. A beat goes by, and Cooper lets out a defeated sigh. "Fine," he mutters.

Helga beckons him to follow her. He rolls his eyes in response, but continues in the direction of his appointment, mumbling, "Whoever came up with the idea of a Brazilian wax should be beaten to death with a stick."

With Cooper out of the room, Jared takes a seat next to me, his soft robe rubbing against my leg.

"You ready for Friday?"

"Sure," I say a little too loud. It's not that I'm nervous. I'm more excited if anything, and I feel good about sharing my body with these two men. I have no doubt Jared won't make things complicated, and Cooper also knows I don't want a relationship.

"I mean, sure." I smile, my tone more even. "I'm all waxed and ready to go."

Jared turns his head to the side and studies me briefly as if assessing something. His perusal makes me nervous, so I blurt out, "Why are you staring at me?"

"Well," he replies inquisitively, "I'm wondering why you don't date."

I give him a mind-your-business look, and he

crosses his arms in front of his chest, his returning gaze indicating that he expects a response.

"Listen, Jared—"

"Don't try to change the topic. I am generally interested, and I'll tell you why after you spill." He leans back in the chair and waits for me to divulge another one of my secrets.

"Fine," I let out a sigh, "but can you keep this between us?" He gives a quick nod, and I continue. "I have no problems with getting a boyfriend, but they've always been sexually ... boring." I really don't want to retell my relationship woes to this man because it's none of his business, but what the hell, I'm intrigued. "You already know about my fetish for porn, so it's understandable that I would want to try every dirty thing that I've already seen. I dated a bunch of losers who weren't sexually compatible with me. It got to the point where I had to give myself orgasms after my partner fell asleep just to satisfy myself. I decided at that point I was better off alone. Why deal with the drama anyway? Sex is what I crave. The emotional attachments tend to be messy."

"Hmm." Jared taps his chin with his index finger. "What if you found someone with an equal appetite to yourself? Would you consider a relationship then?"

I think on his question for a moment, wondering if I actually would take the leap again. My first thought is no, but what if I find someone who wants it as bad as I do? Would I disregard them because of my past experiences? "Are you asking for someone in particular?" I narrow my eyes at him. "Because you are definitely not my type. From what the office girls tell me, you're everyone else's flavor."

Jared shrugs his shoulders. "Don't disagree with you there, but nope, I'm not remotely interested in making you my girlfriend. Now, fucking you is another story." His face splits into a naughty grin. "I do know of someone who might be your perfect match, but I'm thinking you may already know that."

What the? A look of shock and confusion crosses my face. "I have no idea who or what you're talking about." And I really didn't.

"Come on, Beth. You can't be that dense." Jared makes a tsk-tsk sound with his tongue. "Obviously, you and Cooper are a match."

"Umm. Not sure where you're getting that idea from, but I have no interest in him other than physical." Jared rolls his eyes at me. "And I don't appreciate you making this more than what it is."

Holding his hands up in retreat he tells me, "Fine. Just remember this conversation in a few days."

"Ouch!" Both of our heads shoot in the direction of the back toward the piercing scream.

"Oh shit," Jared laughs, "I so don't envy him."

"You are a beast," Cooper yells so loud that the whole Upper East Side probably hears him.

"Should we go back there?" My wide eyes stare at Jared, who is still watching the back room entrance. "Nah. He's been through worse before, and he survived it. He'll be fine."

Raising an eyebrow, I inquire, "What else has he been through?"

Slowly turning his head to face me, Jared shakes his head. "Nope. You made it clear this is completely physical. If you want to know anything about Cooper, ask him."

"Whatever," I mumble as another shout comes from the room. "Could you at least tell me how it is you know Cooper? Though the back and forth banter between you two is hilarious, I feel like the odd woman out. Maybe I want to be in on the joke as well?"

Jared shrugs. "We've been friends for a while." And he ends it at that, the slight lip twitch telling me he isn't going to divulge any more.

Before I get a chance to needle at Jared for being so cagey, Cooper storms in the room. With his face beet red, he glares at both Jared and me. Pointing at both of us he spits, "That was cruel and unusual punishment. Do you know how painful that was? The woman with man hands touched me." I try not to laugh, but Cooper makes it hard.

"Stop acting like a woman and deal with it." Jared chuckles. Standing, he continues, "I'm going to get

47

dressed, and I'll meet you two in a few hours for dinner."

"Screw you," Cooper protests, his fists already clenched at his sides. Jared gives him a three-finger salute and walks to the changing room.

Cooper turns to me with a look of irritation. "Don't ever make me do anything like that again. I've wanted you forever, so I was willing this one time, but no more."

His expression shifts from annoyance to surprise, as if he didn't mean to say the last sentence.

I study him for a beat trying to sense his mood. When I pick up nothing I ask, "What are you talking about?" As I rise from the seat he retreats replying, "Nothing. I'll see you at dinner."

I attempt to grab his arm, but Cooper stalks past me so fast that I don't get close enough to catch him. I'm starting to think it wasn't such a good idea to put him through that. I got so fixated on what I wanted, that I didn't consider how much it might upset him. Then I remember that he and Jared agreed to this, and I wipe the doubt from my mind. I even forget about Cooper's weird statement.

Finally arriving home a while later, I plop onto my couch, and put my feet up on the table. I have a couple of hours to chill before dinner. I'm looking forward to having a meal with the guys in an intimate setting. I think it will add to the foreplay and make us more relaxed for our rendezvous on Friday. Hopefully, by then, Cooper will have calmed down.

Having this downtime is great because it will give me a chance to check in with Carrie. She is a doll, for covering my shift today and the rest of the week. Reaching into my purse, I grab my phone and dial her direct line.

"Hey, bitch," she greets loudly.

"Hey, hon. Aren't you in the office?" I ask, knowing that our boss hates the usage of what he calls "foul language."

"Yup, but Carl the douche is on a call in the conference room, so I can shout as loud as I want and say as many expletives as I like."

Groaning, I ask, "Is Janet there?" She likes to report on us.

"Yes, she is, but she and I have come to an understanding. I get to say cocksucker, fuck, shit, and cunt as much as I want, and I won't tell the boss about her stealing office supplies."

"Wait," I gasp, placing a hand over my mouth. "She steals supplies? But she seems so straight-laced. How the heck did I not see this?"

"Who knows, but I caught her shoving a box of paper into her hatchback during lunch."

"Awesome." I pump my fist to an empty room. "I've been trying to get something on her for months. Do you know that bitch told Carl that I logged onto Facebook too much, and now he monitors my Internet usage closely?"

"Yikes, forgot about that. Well, now we have something on her. I have to figure out how else to use it to our advantage. Anyway, how goes the threesome prep?"

"It's going really good." I lean against the pillow on the couch and rub the back of my neck with the palm of my hand. "We went to the spa today and got primped and pampered. Cooper didn't take well to the waxing, but he'll get over it."

"That's hilarious. What about the other one? Jared, right?"

"Yeah." I laugh as I think about how at ease he is with everything. "He's apparently a pro at being taken care of by women."

"I bet, but let's go back to Cooper for a sec. The blond cutie freaked? That surprises me. From how you described him, he doesn't seem the type."

Letting out a sigh I tell her, "I think there's more than meets the eye to him. And listen to this; Jared thinks that I should try to date him. Crazy, right?"

"Really …"

The sarcastic way she says the word gives me pause. "What the hell did you use that tone for?"

"Tone. Me?" Her voice mocks surprise, and her indifference is annoying.

"Stop being an ass and tell me what you meant."

Carrie chuckles, decreeing, "I think Jared is onto something. You haven't been dating much. If he's not interested, then why not Cooper?"

"Seriously? There are too many reasons to count. First off, I barely know him."

"Yet, you plan on sleeping with him and his friend, I might add."

"Yeah, so?" I murmur like a child unable to prove a point. "He likes to sleep around. He even told me so."

"Hmm … someone with the same sexual appetite as yourself. I don't see a problem there."

Rolling my eyes, I try to come up with some other excuse, but nothing materializes in my mind. I respond the only way I know how when I lose an argument. "Whatever, Carrie." I twirl my finger around a lock of my hair, frustration making me tug it a bit too hard.

"Just what I thought." She laughs. "So when are you going to make a move on him, and I'm not just talking about the sex?"

"Don't know if that's a good idea." I sigh. "Things are already complicated with Jared involved, and they've been friends for a while. I don't want to mess with that."

"Wait, what?" she says, her tone filled with surprise. "Did they apply for the ad at the same time? That would be the only way you'd get them both."

"That's probably what happened," I answer, still

pissed at myself for not telling her about the agency. "Anyway, I asked Jared about it, but he's being cagey. And you know what else?" I bite my bottom lip before continuing. "Something about them both seems familiar. I knew of Jared but never saw him up close until the coffee shop. In the case of Cooper, I've never met him before. Nothing in his file says I should even know the guy."

"Yeah, that is weird," Carrie, agrees. "We'll come back to that later though. What's important is the dress that you're wearing today. You have to drive both of them wild."

"I love how you gloss over important issues to talk about clothing."

"It's a gift. Now tell me about the outfit."

"Fine," I groan. "I found this amazing Bardot dress at Bloomingdale's with matching strappy heels for a steal. Gimme a sec, and I'll send you a picture." I scroll through my phone, searching for the screenshot I took the other day and text it to Carrie.

"Holy shit, girl, that is hot. Put your hair up and no heavy makeup."

"All right," I agree, standing. "I have to get dressed, *chica*. I'll call you after dinner and let you know how things go."

"You better," she demands. "See ya."

After hanging up, I walk into my room, the entire time thinking about Cooper. There is something about him I can't put my finger on. Maybe at tonight's dinner, I'll figure it out.

I smile at the thought of sharing a meal with both of them, knowing it will only add to the pleasure of what's to come. Soon, I tell myself. I'll get to experience something that I've wanted forever, and I know these men will make it awesome.

CHAPTER 5

Don't Play with Your Food

COOPER

Jared: You alive?

I RECEIVE Jared's text an hour after I get back to my apartment. My body hurts like a motherfucker. Especially the spots where that she-devil of a man-beast tore away my hair. My dick still shrivels up at the thought of that warm liquid she spread near it. A normal person would have said no to waxing, especially if, like me, they've never done it before, but I could never deny Beth what she wanted.

For a long time, I ignored the part of me that cared for her, shutting my mind off to those feelings. It was the only way I knew how to survive. Perhaps that's the real reason I fell for my ex. My mind was completely filled with everything about her, allowing me to forget all about Beth. Now that she's here in my life again, I can't even remember how I lasted so long without her.

Me: Barely.

I search the fridge for a beer, finding it immediately. I need to relax before our dinner tonight. I'm not sure why she wanted to eat with us in the first place, but I go with it. Beth mentioned earlier that she'd be taking us to a swanky Asian fusion restaurant called Buddakan, located on the west side near Fourteenth Street. The only places I usually visit on that side of town are the Highline Elevated Park and the Apple Store. This will be the first time I go to a restaurant in that area, and I'm looking forward to it. I've heard good things about this place, and the menu looks appetizing.

The soothing sound of my opening beer relaxes me as I take a seat on my couch. Due to the sensitivity after waxing, I groan as my ass hits the cushion. My phone buzzes in my hand, notifying me of another incoming text.

Jared: So I did something ...

I let out a sigh and take a sip of my beer.

Me: What?

Jared: I merely mentioned to Beth that you two should date.

Damn near spitting my drink out, I dial Jared, setting my beer on the table at the same time. It rings twice and then his carefree voice comes through.

"Can you explain to me the reason behind your outing me?" I ask, resting my face in my hand. "Because I distinctly remember us having a shut the fuck up conversation."

"You really need to relax, Coop. She shot me down anyway."

"She did?" My response sounds pained, so I clear my throat to cover it up. "I mean, good. I'm not interested in her either."

Jared laughs at the other end of the line. "That reply was about as subtle as a freight train."

"Fuck you," I spit, not angry with him, just pissed that she wouldn't even consider being with me. In reality, it makes sense. To her, I'm a stranger who was matched with her via a dating agency, but to me she is everything. I can't blame her for being skittish.

"That was harsh," Jared says, his mirth still prevalent. "But I wasn't finished."

"She said no, so what more is there to say?"

"God, you really suck at women." He laughs again. "This is why I succeed in all my endeavors, business and extracurricular. I'm an expert at reading people, women especially, and most importantly, I know how to please them. If I remember correctly, I gave you a few pointers back in the day."

"Yeah, whatever," I reply, putting my feet up on the couch. He never lets me forget about the times he had to show me what to do in the bedroom. Not with each other, of course, because we are both into women. Before Brittany, Jared and I often ended up sharing the same girl from time to time. He was a great teacher and would instruct me on ways to make the woman's experience with us memorable. He was the one who made me feel comfortable with myself, and probably the cause of my constant appetite. "So, you were saying?" I ask, remembering some of those crazy sex-fueled times, silently hoping that Beth and I can make our own.

"Before you bite my head off," Jared starts again, "I'll let you in on a few things. Women are a contradiction of feelings. Many deny themselves, choosing instead to ignore their inner wants and needs. This is where I come in. I give anyone who shares my bed the tools necessary to release their invisible restraints, and the results are always spectacular."

"You sound like a yoga guru," I mutter, reaching for my beer and taking another swig.

"Maybe I am. I find when I'm able to tap into the part of a woman, she voluntarily cages, I'm freeing her from a drab life."

"What does this have to do with Beth?" I ask him, generally curious about the philosophical connection Jared is trying to make.

"Beth is like foil."

"Foil?" I chuckle. "I think she'd take offense to that."

"Maybe," he laughs, "but hear me out."

"Go on, guru."

"When you tear off a sheet, it's flat and smooth with no real dimension. If you ball that same piece of foil up, it becomes a hard, impenetrable mass that can only be separated without tearing by delicate hands. Beth is that ball right now, and as soon as she opens up, new grooves and intricacies that weren't on the original sheet will be prominent, allowing her to be who she really wants to be. Consider me the first set of hands peeling back her layers. By planting the idea of you in her head, she'll be forced to think about the what ifs with you only. I've made it clear that I don't want her in that way. And let's be honest, if you told me not to take part in sleeping with her, I'd honor that request. My dick might get mad at me, but I always have other options."

I think about what Jared just said to me. He has an interesting way of explaining things, but in the end, they always make sense. I'm hoping this plan of his works because I want her bad.

"Uhh. Am I supposed to say thank you then?"

"Nah. Like I always tell you, I owe you my life. Anything I can do to get you two together, I will, though we will have to eventually tell her who we really are. I don't think she'll be pissed … much."

"I hope not."

"Have to get dressed for dinner. Catch you later."

"See you, man." I end the call, now filled with a smidgen of hope for what's to come.

Later that evening, I arrive at Buddakan first. As soon as I walk through the door, the scents of mouth-watering Asian cuisine hit me. I've already seen the menu and can't wait to try an entrée.

The decor is incredible, with its cream-colored walls, high ceilings, and extravagant chandeliers. It's a wonder that my ex didn't make me take her to this place before. The pricing seems up her alley. She never offered to pay or split the bill ever. It's not that I couldn't afford to take her out; it was merely the thought that counted. This is one of the reasons why Bethany is such a wonderful woman. She offered to take Jared and me to this restaurant, not expecting either of us to foot the bill. Perhaps she felt as though she owed us something. Dinner between the participating individuals is not a requirement to be filled prior to consummation. In fact, everything that we've done so far isn't necessary at all.

Beth has always been kind like that. I could tell she had a big heart from the moment I saw her, and her smile could melt the polar ice caps. She had me wrapped around her finger and didn't even know it. I have to tell her everything, eventually, but for now I'm going to keep quiet until absolutely necessary.

"How may I help you, sir?" the host asks, bringing me out of my musings.

"I'm," I check my watch, "about ten minutes early. Phillips, party of three."

"Ah." He nods. "We received a call from a Mr. Carrington. He said to tell you that he had a late meeting and couldn't attend. He also said to tell you, umm ... you're welcome."

I shake my head. Only Jared would do something along these lines.

Pulling out my phone, I shoot him a quick thank you text but decide not to check the response.

"Right this way, sir."

After following the host through the dining area, he pauses at a tiny cream table with a sleek decorative lamp that has a square shade sitting on top. Since the lighting of the dining room is dim, this makes sense. Most restaurants use candles when faced with lighting issues, but with the design of this place, a candle would probably lessen the beauty.

"Have a seat, sir. Your waiter, Charles, will be with you shortly."

Nodding, because apparently, that's all I can do these past few minutes, I take my seat. When Charles finally arrives at my table, I order a glass of the house Chardonnay to calm my nerves. I've never been alone with Beth like this, so I'm bound to have foot in mouth disease at least once while I speak to her. About five or ten minutes pass by before Beth is brought over by another hostess. It feels like it took an eternity for her to get here, but as soon as I see her, I forget why I was so nervous in the first place.

Breathtaking is the only way to describe how this woman looks tonight. I don't know where she bought her black dress from, but as soon as I find out, I'm buying stock in the company.

The shell of the garment accentuates the curve of her hips and the shape of her breasts, the lace overlay adding to the mystique of her figure. My eyes trail up and down her, pausing mid-thigh, causing me to zero in on her bare legs. I can't wait to run my fingers along her smooth skin, eventually getting them in between her legs. I love it when she puts her hair up like she has today. It reminds me of the first time I saw her that way. God, she is so fucking beautiful, and I want to pounce on her. Of course, my dick wholeheartedly agrees.

"Miss?"

She turns around to face the hostess, and holy mother of God, all the blood rushes from my brain to my already aching dick. I imagine myself pulling down the zipper slowly; the sound of the metal would drive me insane. And Jesus Christ, the ass on her. I'm going to need to claim that shit in the next couple of days.

"Okay, thanks." She finishes up with the hostess and turns around. I have no idea what was said in the past few minutes because I was focused on other things.

Taking her seat, she asks me, "Jared isn't coming?"

"Appears not," I say, feigning calm. I signal the waiter over to order another glass of Chardonnay. Before he arrives, I ask, "What's your poison this evening?" She grins, licking her plump lips. I don't believe she meant it to be sexy, but my eyes drop to her mouth, focusing on the sultry way her tongue moves. What I wouldn't give to trace the tip of mine along the seam of that mouth. I take a huge gulp, finishing the last of my wine when the waiter arrives.

"Another glass, sir?" I nod, my gaze still focused on her.

"And you, Miss?" he asks her.

"I'll have the same."

The server departs, and there's a beat of silence between us until she breaks it.

"So, I guess it's just you and me," she says, stating the obvious. Her face appears nervous and she fidgets a little.

"Is there something wrong with that?" My voice is low and sensual because I'm trying to get a reaction out of her.

"No, of course not," she replies, her tone equally as breathy. "I am disappointed. I thought it would be good for all of us to relax before Friday, and what better way to do that than a candlelight dinner."

"Hmm … I see your point, but you're forgetting something." Leaning forward I reach out to touch her face running my fingers slowly along the smooth skin of her cheek, my thumb pausing at her sexy mouth. I want to kiss her so badly, and the hitch in her breath tells me she wants it too. How did this go from zero to one hundred in a matter of moments? "You don't need both of us to, as you say, relax. I'm just as capable as he is of relieving any tension you might have. Would you like me to show you?"

Smiling, I give her a challenging look, daring her to make a move. Her eyes go wide as she thinks about what I just said. My lower half is tender from the experience at the salon earlier, but my mouth and hands work just fine.

She pauses before responding to my suggestion. I

almost glide my hand down somewhere I shouldn't in public until she says, "It's probably not a good idea since Jared isn't here. I want to experience both of you together for the first time and maybe afterward we can explore your ability to remove tension."

I smirk, and then incline my head to study her. Beth's eyes are filled with erotic heat, burning so hot; it causes my erection to go rigid. Everything about this woman turns me on. It's like she's the remote control connected to my dick—the sway of her hips, her sexy tits, and that mouth, the power button that brings it to attention.

The waiter returns with our drinks order and then proceeds to take our entrée selections. I order the black pepper beef rib eye steak, while she orders the Alaskan black cod.

While we wait for the food, she takes a sip of her drink and asks, "Are you ever going to tell me how you and Jared know each other?"

I knew this was coming, but I'm still not prepared to tell her. How do you let someone know you've wanted them for years, that you've fantasized about a moment like this so often it became real in your mind? I don't want to come off as a crazy stalker because I'm not. I didn't follow her, and I don't have creepy pictures hanging on the wall. What I do have, though, is a long memory.

"Why is that so important you?" I ask, not really interested, but stalling.

"I always feel like you and Jared have these silent conversations, and I want to be a part of them. I think if I know your history, then we could connect more as individuals, and it might heighten the effect of our experience."

"I'm all for increased pleasure, Beth, but I'm not ready to let you in on that part of myself. Let's just say me and Jared have been friends for many years, and he's helped me through a lot of tough times."

She bites her lip as if contemplating whether she should continue with her line of questioning. A small part of me just wants to say fuck it and tell her my real name, and how I've been in love with her since I was sixteen. That might freak her out though, especially since she only saw me once in high school. I doubt she would remember the scrawny kid with glasses and a huge nose. An injury, plastic surgery, and a whole life-style change courtesy of Jared made me the man I am today, so what does it matter who I was back then?

"That's not really an answer," she replies, rolling her eyes. "I'm sure there are plenty more details."

"Maybe," I smile coyly, "but you'll have to wait until I'm good and ready to give them to you."

"What if you're never ready? What do I do then?" Her piercing stare is so powerful; I almost buckle under the pressure. However, I remain steadfast, reminding myself that I'm so close to having her.

"Let's make a deal, Beth. Go out with me on a real date, and I'll tell you anything you want."

"Isn't this a real date?"

I shake my head. "Nope. This is more of a pre-meeting, and it was initially supposed to include Jared. I'll take you on our own date at another time of my choosing."

Beth lets out an exaggerated sigh and it's too cute. "Okay, fine. But you have to tell me everything, and I mean it. I want your deepest, darkest secrets, Cooper Whitmore."

Grinning, I nod just as dinner arrives. We eat in silence for most of the meal, with the occasional small talk about her job and my son. By the time dessert comes around we decide to call it a night. I escort her to the cab first, giving her a kiss on the cheek. I want a real lip lock, but change my mind at the last minute. I'll have more chances on Friday, and plan to take advantage of all of them.

As I ride home in the cab, I think back to the accident that changed my life. Jared and I had been fooling around somewhere. I don't even remember the name of the place. It happened the summer before senior year. There was a spot near the cliffs where kids would swing on a rope and fall into the water—a place fairly popular with the teenage crowd in our town.

That summer, it had been particularly hot. I don't recall if it was considered a drought, I just remember wanting to cool off that day. Jared suggested that we go to the point, and I agreed. When we arrived, there was no one in the area, so no usual line. Jared and I flipped a coin to see who would go first because as teenagers it made sense at the time. I distinctly remember feeling uneasy about jumping in, but I shook it off. To create momentum, I ran as fast as I could, catching the rope in my hand, and swinging in one swift motion. As soon as I let go of the rope I knew that I was in trouble. Instead of falling into a deep body of water, usually eight to twelve feet, I fell into a shallow pool of considerably less. There were some spots where the jagged rock protruded from the river, which wouldn't have normally been there, had it been at the proper level. Upon landing, I broke my leg in three places, had some broken ribs, and one of the rocks somehow managed to score across my nose. The cut was so deep that I needed to have reconstructive surgery. The doctor ended up giving me a nose job that I am ever so grateful for. After the surgery, I looked completely different.

Jared felt like shit afterward, so he reinstated his mission to "remake me" if you will. He'd brought it up at the end of our junior year, but with finals and other school commitments, it was put on hold. He gave me pointers on sex. I lifted weights and became a little more polished. I ended up being homeschooled my senior year because of the broken bones and recovery time. I never saw Beth again.

The taxicab arrives at my apartment, and I get out after paying. As I walk to the front door, I think about how much my life has changed, and how lucky I am to have a second chance with this woman. I'm eagerly looking forward to experiencing everything with her. Two more days and, she'll be mine.

CHAPTER 6

Three's A Crowd

JARED

I CONSIDER MYSELF A CALM MAN, never letting anything get to me. Cooper, on the other hand, is a ball of nerves. I haven't seen him this unglued since high school.

It started when he called me the morning after their dinner. He kept going on about how he just wanted to tell her and how shitty he felt about lying. I told him to calm the fuck down and continue with our charade until after, reminding him of what's coming next. I didn't spend time in a sex shop picking out toys for him to back out now. I understand his reluctance to let the lie continue, but I have faith it will all work itself out. To give him more time to work his shit out, I offered to install the sex swing in the hotel, as well as get everything else ready. I asked Cooper to meet me there at six, while Beth isn't due to arrive until eight. It made sense for him to arrive at an earlier time. Apparently, my thirty-one-year-old friend needs a pep talk.

A knock at the door signals the arrival of our attendant Ben, Brian, Bob or whatever the fuck his name is. I'd called down to the front desk for extra towels, and he'd offered to bring them personally. Usually the maid staff are the ones who complete that task, however Brice insisted.

"Here are your towels, Mr. Carrington," Bray offers. He shoots a quick glance over my shoulder as if looking for someone.

Clearing my throat, I garner his attention again. "Did you need something else, Byron?" I give him a pointed look and wait for a response.

"Bradley, sir," he corrects me. After hesitating for a beat, he then blurts, "I was wondering if Mr. Whitmore would be arriving today." His blush is obvious, and it makes me curious what the hell Cooper did to get this room.

"He'll be here in about twenty minutes." I give him an honest response because I'm generally interested in what he'll say next. "Did you want to wait for him?" Biting his bottom lip as a sign of contemplation, Barry lets out a sigh and nods.

I step to the side, allowing him to enter the room. Then, I toss the towels on the side table, near the entrance. Who knows when and where we'll need to wipe up.

"You can wait right there." I point to the red chair in the seating area. Heading to the bedroom, I continue to prep for our night, placing the sex toys on the nightstand and securing the sex swing perpendicular to the bed. Cooper was able to have a ladder left in the room for installation. I thought about attaching it above the bed, but logistically, it seemed to make more sense here.

Toys. Check.

Lube. Check.

It all appears to be in order. The only thing left is to make sure that Cooper has his shit together.

A murmur of voices draws me out of the bedroom and into the living room. It's there I see Cooper in a close conversation with Barney. I take a moment to study my friend before approaching. Outwardly he appears calm to most, but I know him all too well. The slight sheen of sweat on his forehead and the tapping of his hand against his leg are telltale signs that he's nervous. Boris here isn't making things any easier by crowding him. I'm not sure exactly what he wants, but it's definitely time to get rid of the pest.

"Hey, Coop," I greet him as I enter. He gives me a distracted chin lift, turning back to whatever Bogard is saying. The attendant is speaking so low that I can barely hear anything. I clear my throat to gain Bing's attention. This seems to be the only thing that works with the guy

"Have you finished with my friend?" Crossing my arms in front of my chest, I give him an annoyed glare. "Because we need to get the night's festivities underway." Benton frowns at me. I was fine with him waiting before, but the conversation appears to be agitating Cooper, so Bison has to go.

"I'm almost done, sir," Brody gives a stuttered response.

"No. I think you're done, Beauford," I growl. Cooper shakes his head, smirking at me.

"That's Bradley, sir," Benjamin says, his tone uneasy. "I only wanted to ask Mr. Whitmore if he—"

I make a slashing motion with my hand shutting down Bruce. I catch a hint of petulance on his face, but he backs away, turns, and strides toward the exit.

"What was that about?"

Cooper smiles. "He was in the process of asking me on a date, but you embarrassed him."

"I don't even want to know."

"Wasn't going to tell you."

As Butch yanks the door open, a startled Beth stands in the doorway wearing … Oh shit. She obviously came with her "A" game because this woman has on a brown trench coat with black heels, and my guess is nothing under it. My dick says hello as I scan her body.

Bernard says something before he leaves, but I pay no attention. Cooper has obviously seen her, but he makes no move to approach. Licking his lips, he stares at her in awe and worship, as if playing out in his mind how he will consume her.

She saunters in the room with confidence. The delicious sway of her hips makes my already hard cock turn into steel.

"I thought I'd make access …" she pauses, "… easy."

With that statement, she removes her jacket and lets it fall to the floor. My breath hitches as I stare at her naked body. She has an amazing figure, with her curves and legs that go on forever. I often wondered if the hair on her pussy would match the red on her head, but I guess I'll never know because Beth decided to go bare for us. I want to go and palm her breast, lick her nipple, or something, but I'm waiting to see what Cooper does first.

"Where do you want me?"

CHAPTER 7

Insert Point A Into Slot B

COOPER

WHERE DO I WANT HER? Is she serious? Fuck, I'd take her anywhere.

The sensual tone of the woman I've spent a long time fantasizing about sends a signal straight to my dick that it's on. The nerves from earlier disappear with her one sentence, and the inner sex god who has been in hiding the past few days comes out to play.

The two strides it takes to reach her feel like an eternity, but as soon as I'm right in front of her, I reach out and run my knuckles across her cheek. She bites her lip in response and grins.

The sounds of "I'll Make Love to You" by Boyz II Men fill the room, and I damn near roll my eyes at Jared's selection. Doesn't he realize that no one listens to music when they have sex, or at least I don't? The sounds of moaning and groaning are usually my melody.

"I'm thinking we can start here."

I kiss her, hard, wanting to devour her at every turn. Her body surrenders to me immediately as she leans into the lip lock. The proverbial fireworks go off in my mind as she wraps her hand around my neck, pulling me close. I groan at the delicious contact her nipples make with my covered chest, their hardness a sign of her arousal. Being with Beth like this is like a dream come true, and so much more.

"Take her to the bedroom," Jared rasps from the other side of the living room, the sounds of footsteps coming closer. For that one moment we kissed, I forgot that he was even in the room, the power of our lips coming together send my mind into an erotic tail-spin I never want to escape.

Grasping her hand, I guide Beth to the bedroom. The first thing I notice is the muted light of the candles on each nightstand. They illuminate the different types of sex toys he purchased earlier in the week. I'm not quite sure what each does, but

I'm a fast learner. Beth lets go of my hand to explore the sexual wonderland that Jared has created, starting with the swing that I now realize is perpendicular to the king size mattress. My dick twitches in my pants as I observe her running a finger along the straps of the swing. She then moves to each nightstand, inspecting the different sex toys. A huge grin spreads across her face as she catches sight of the oval-shaped device with the floral design.

"Mmm," she moans, continuing to caress the toy. "I've always wanted to try this one."

"I have it on good authority that it will get you off in two minutes or less," Jared rumbles from behind me, the timbre of his voice filled with desire. "I thought you would at least have your shirt off at this point, Coop. I think our guest would prefer some skin, wouldn't you?"

Nodding, but not turning to face him, I unbutton my blue Oxford dress shirt, my normally dexterous fingers, unsteady. As she watches me undress with rapt attention, I get bold when I reach my pants, purposefully removing the belt at a slow and sensual pace, undoing the button, and then finally gliding the zipper down. I make quick work of my shoes and allow my pants to hit the floor. She licks her lips as if some sort of approval, causing me to feel like a god and her my disciple. The hunger in her eyes rises to new heights, and when I finally get down to my boxer briefs, I stop.

"Come here," I beckon her because I want to feel her lips again. She shakes her head no, testing my resolve, but I will not have this woman deny me.

Ever.

"I think she's trying to play hard to get. Don't you, Jared?" My statement is brazen, and though I can't see Jared's face, I know it surprises him too. He's usually the vocal leader when we occasionally share women, but with her, I can't control my want and need for her.

"Yes, she is," Jared agrees, the rustling sound behind me, a sign that he's removing his clothing as well.

I give him a few beats to finish, and then I tell him, "Bring her to me, so I can show her who's really in charge, will ya, Jared?"

"Sure." A now boxer clad Jared saunters by me and grabs her by the forearm, playfully tugging her in my direction. He presents her to me like the Christmas present I've always wanted. As my eyes trail up and down her body, I make a quick decision that I know what will excite her, and pleasure Jared and me at the same time. First, I wrap my hands around her waist, pulling her into another erotic kiss, eventually taking her hard nipple into my mouth. Jared takes this opportunity to palm her other breast from behind and drag his tongue along her throat. Her core grinds against my erection, but I'm not giving that to her. Yet.

Breaking away from the kiss, I gently force her to her knees. After all, she told me no, and she deserves to be punished.

"You disobeyed me. Show me how sorry you are." Pulling my cock out of my boxers, I shoot a quick glance up at Jared, give him a brisk nod, and he releases his dick too. I damn near come in my pants as she runs a finger along her clit, slowly, being sure to cover it in her wetness. I go rock hard when she takes that finger and spreads her erotic juices along my cock, stroking it in the process.

"Fuck," I groan as I thrust, my hardness moving in and out of her fist. I glance over at Jared, who is stroking himself in time with her movements.

"This feels amazing," I gasp, "but I think you owe some attention to Jared. Go suck his cock, but don't get too comfortable because mine will need attention again."

Like the sexual creature she is, Beth obeys, reaching out to grab Jared's waiting erection. Her mouth immediately latches on, sucking and pumping his dick into submission. When it appears as if he can't take anymore, she releases him with a pop and comes back to me, taking my dick in her mouth so deep that she practically gags. I grab her by the hair and fuck her face, then yank her off and force her to go back to sucking Jared's dick. The action is visceral and erotic, but I want more.

Pulling her off Jared's cock again, I bend over and give her a blistering kiss. I'm so filled with lust, I don't even care that I taste my friend on her lips. "Bed," I order as I break our kiss, getting tired of the back and forth. I want to taste that sweet wet pussy of hers and this current position doesn't allow it.

With satisfying speed, Beth climbs onto the king-size bed and rests her back against the mattress. At some point tonight, I'll want her on all fours,

"Usually," Jared growls, "I like to be the one in charge." Jared eyes Beth, who is now pleasuring herself with her fingers, leisurely thrusting the middle one in and out of her wet heat. "But I'll do this for you this one time."

"I know," I agree as my arousal screams at me to take her. "Understand this, Jared. After tonight, I won't ever share her again. With you or anyone else." Chancing a glance at him, I catch the slightest lip twitch.

"Figured as much." No other words of friendship and camaraderie are exchanged after this. My mind switches back to all the things I've ever dreamed of doing with this woman.

Turning my attention back to her, in a low sensual tone I say, "I didn't tell you that you could touch yourself, my sweet Beth. Give me your naughty hand." Wisely obeying, she gives me a wicked grin as I crawl on the bed next to her, Jared on the opposite side. I take her two fingers and suck the wetness off. Her pussy tastes like cherries, ecstasy, and mine. I know that as soon as I wrap my lips around her clit, I won't ever leave.

"Such a bad girl," I scold, after letting her wrist go. She reaches out to grab my dick, but I grip her wrists, explaining, "Girls who don't listen only get pleasure from one of us." Jared takes my unspoken cue, spreading her legs and attaching his mouth to her pussy. She calls out his name as his expert tongue plunges in and out, her shouts getting louder the closer he gets to her sensitive nub.

Propping my elbow on the bed, I watch as Jared begins to suck on her clit, the entire time stroking myself. I want to get in there but the scene between Jared and Beth is so fucking hot and mesmerizing that I can't move.

"Cooper," she moans, "let me suck your cock again, please."

I almost tell her no, but the guttural tone of the word please changes my mind. I crawl on top of her, straddling her face. She gives me a slow stroke before running her tongue along the base of me to the tip. My dick slips in between her lips with ease, the vibrations of her moans nearly make me come. Her mouth engulfs me, her nonexistent gag reflex causing my eyes to roll back into my head. This woman doesn't realize how much power she has over my arousal and eventual release. If I let her take control for too long, then I'm done for.

"My turn to taste her," I rumble. Withdrawing from her mouth, I move down the bed, forcing Jared to switch places with me. He responds with a grunt, taking his place over her face.

After slipping my tongue inside her pussy, I get a burst of the cherry flavor again, this time with a hint of vanilla. I damn near lose my mind at her erotic flavor, and it's taking every ounce of my control not to fuck her. I slip two fingers inside as I continue to lick her, her hips rocking in time with my hands. I fucking love pleasuring her.

"Get me one of the toys," I demand Jared who is in his own state of sexual bliss. I don't think that he hears me at first, but after an extra two pumps in her mouth, he pulls out and does as I ask.

"This one." Jared hands me an oval-shaped device that has what appears to be a small suction cup on the opposite side. "The clerk called it the Womanizer, and it works really well." He gives me a quick explanation on how to use it, smiling the entire time. "I think we can give her multiple orgasms with this."

"Good. Cuff her to the bed. We don't want her getting any ideas about touching that pussy again."

Her body shivers at the mention of restraints, but she remains obedient. The handcuff purchase was a surprise. Jared sent me a photo of them earlier asking if he could introduce them. I initially declined, but changed my mind, asking him to hide them in the drawer. I'm so glad I did, because fuck me, the sight of her writhing in pleasure is going to shatter me.

Jared cuffs Beth's left wrist to the tiny slot at the headboard, while I attach the right, being sure to place pillows under her head for elevation. I leave her legs free for what I have planned.

Her breaths become shallow as I run my tongue along the underside of her right breast. Jared mimics my movement on the other side, and I wish he would stop. I want access to both of her sexy tits.

"I want you," she groans, struggling and squirming beneath us, "both."

Squeezing her center with my other hand, I shush her and tell Jared, "She's missing your cock, Jared. Go and give her what she wants, will you?"

Nodding, he sucks her nipple one last time before straddling her face again. Even though I can't see her, I know Jared's cock is already in her mouth based on his groan, and the movement of his hips.

With that taken care of, I go back to my plan. Spreading her legs apart, I give her one last lick, relishing in the flavor of her wetness. Her hips buck against my mouth, but I hold her down, needing her to be steady while I do this. "I'm going to need you to be still, baby." I kiss the inside of her thighs to calm her, though the quivering of her legs tells me she's barely hanging on by a thread.

"You seemed to be fascinated with this particular device." I glide it along her legs, so she can feel what it is, separating her pussy, exposing the sensitive nub. After I fit the miniature suction cup snugly over her clit, I turn it on. Immediately, she yanks at her cuffs in frustration as her hips writhe in pleasure. I bet she'd scream my name if her mouth wasn't full. I'm so turned on I need to stroke myself.

Using some of the juices from her wet pussy, I rub them all over my dick, which is so damn hard it's painful. "So good," I groan, fucking my hand. I want to be inside of her so bad, but not yet.

Patience, I tell myself as I continue to jerk off. I'm close to—

"Fuck, Coop, I can't hold on much longer. Gotta come."

"No," I snarl, continuing to pump my dick. "Only I get to come in her mouth."

Jared releases a frustrating groan as he pulls out, but I don't give a fuck. He can use her to the point of release, hell, I'll probably even let him fuck her, but only my cum goes inside her mouth. I want to be the first man to shoot down her throat, even though I'm letting Jared have her in this way.

He goes to the right side of her and begins to stroke himself, the aim of his dick directly over her tits. Beth's erotic sounds are now audible, and it's so damn hot.

The stroking goes on for a few more beats, our pleasure eventually hitting its peak. Then, as if we planned it, we all come together. First, her body stiffens, and she comes, Jared shoots his release on her tits immediately after, and I end the cycle with ropes of my hot cum landing on her pussy.

After my last spurt, I use my dick to rub it all over her inner thigh and on the outside of her, simultaneously turning off and removing the vibrator with my other hand. Based on her moans, I know she wants more, but with Jared collapsed next to her, and my cock semi-hard, it might take a minute for us to start again.

"Jared, uncuff her. I'll go get a towel to clean up." Rising from the bed, he grunts in response.

"You okay up there?" I grin at Beth. Her face is flushed, and she has a sheen of sweat all over her body. She doesn't answer. Instead, her eyes trail down to my dick, which might I add, is still spreading cum in between her legs. It's funny because I didn't realize I was doing it.

"I'm good." Her response is breathy. "Actually, great. The better question would be how are you doing? I only ask because your dick seems to want more friction at the moment."

She's able to sit up from her original position since

Jared has removed the cuffs, so she takes this opportunity to grip me. I knock her hand away so that I can go about getting a warm washcloth.

"Be right back, baby." I lean forward and give her a quick kiss. "We're not done yet."

After entering the bathroom, I glance into the mirror and have no idea who I'm looking at. My hair is mussed, and I have a smug look on my face. I've never been that dominant in bed, but with her, it's so fucking natural, like breathing.

Giving myself a quick pep talk, because the fucking nerves are beginning to rear their annoying head, I splash of water on my face. With cloth in hand and a little more swagger in my step, I'm ready to rock Beth's world.

BETHANY

OH. My. Shit.

That was the best experience of sexual pleasure I have ever had in my entire life. None of my other encounters have come even close to what just happened. Jared's cock in my mouth, that delicious vibrator, and Cooper in control of it all was just … I don't have any words to describe it.

Currently, I'm basking in the glow of my orgasm while Cooper is in the bathroom grabbing a cloth. The dirty girl in me wants to remain sticky with their cum, but I know I'll have another helping of it soon. To pass the time I make small conversation with Jared. There's something I want to ask him before Cooper returns, and perhaps in his sexed-out state he may answer.

"What's the deal tonight? I thought you were the alpha in this duo."

Shrugging his shoulders, Jared gives me a lazy grin, revealing, "I worked it out with Coop earlier. Never seen him like this with any other woman, though." He gives me a pointed look as if trying to tell me something with his eyes, and before I get a chance to question him on it, Cooper comes back in the room.

After handing Jared a warm cloth, he takes a seat next to me, wiping down the remnants of our earlier acts. He does this gently, first trailing it along my breast. The combination of the wetness and air cause my nipples to stiffen, so he takes advantage, sucking them hard. I moan at his ministrations as he uses one hand to massage and lick my tits, the other gliding the cloth along my stomach.

When he reaches the apex of my thighs, he releases my breast and says, "The carnal part of me wants to leave my cum on your pussy, where it belongs." He wipes himself away. "But I think it will be more fun to mark my territory from the inside, don't you?"

Glancing down, I notice he's hard again. My pussy quivers at the thought of him doing dirty things to me.

Reaching over my head, he grabs something. I can't quite see what it is because he passes it over to Jared.

"We need to get her ready for both of us," Cooper rumbles. "She seems to like you licking her pussy, Jared, so get on with it." He then leans against the headboard stroking his cock.

Looming over me, Jared gives another one of his filthy grins, waving the glass plug in front of my face. He slides it across my lips, ordering, "Suck."

Eagerly, I open my mouth, letting my lips envelop the toy, and follow his command. He trails kisses along my breast, eventually reaching my sex. I moan when he slips a finger inside, thrusting slow and teasingly.

Grabbing my wrist, Cooper squeezes some lube into my palm, guiding me to his cock. I stroke him in time with Jared's fingers.

"Fuck. She's so wet, Coop," Jared groans.

"I bet she is," he growls, thrusting his hardness in my rigid grip.

Moments later Cooper gently tugs the plug from in between my lips and hands it to Jared, who wastes no time easing it in my dark crevice. The feeling is foreign at first, but as Jared begins to move it, a myriad of pleasurable sensations hit me. He uses one hand to work my pussy and the other to rotate the plug.

"So good," I sigh as I continue to stroke Cooper. My hand falls away as he changes position. Jared adjusts to his shift, removing his fingers from inside me, but leaving the plug inside.

Now lying on his back, Cooper grabs me by the waist, dragging me up his legs, and rests my bottom on his upper thighs. He runs his fingers along my crack, pausing when he reaches the plug.

"In a second, I'm going to pull this out and claim your ass. Jared is taking your pussy." My body shivers at his words. "I'll try to be gentle, but I've been dying to fuck you all night."

I gasp as Cooper eases the plug from my ass, tossing it on the bed. He lifts me and lines himself up with my forbidden passageway, his soft tip immediately penetrating my tight ring. I groan at the slow burn of his shallow thrust as his cock goes deeper, claiming me.

"Oh fuck," he growls. "She's so damn tight, Jared." His breaths are ragged as he continues to enter me, the sensation of his plunges taking me to new heights. "Get over here, Jared." Cooper stills. "This is too good, and I'm not going to last."

Jared takes his place in between us, rubbing the crown of his dick along my wet center. Not wasting any time, he slides inside, causing me to feel completely full.

Splaying my back against Cooper's chest, my body

melts, allowing them both to move inside me. A feeling of complete ecstasy comes over me when Jared and Cooper's rhythm begins to match. An orgasm from deep within begins to build, and I'm afraid. I sense the shattering power behind it.

"Beth, you feel so fucking good," Cooper moans. "Wanted this for so long."

"God, her pussy is sweet, Coop. Need to fuck her harder," Jared says through gritted teeth.

"Do it," I pant, bracing for what's coming next.

My orgasm hits me without warning, and it's like I'm on another plane of existence. I feel both of their cocks ravaging me, and I fucking love it. I've never experienced anything so good. I sense the first throb of release as my ass fills with all that is Cooper. Seconds later, Jared comes, his seed seeping out of my pussy. I try to ride it out with them, but my mind and body are so shattered, I pass out.

JARED

"WHAT A NIGHT," I yawn, joining Cooper at the breakfast bar. He hands me a cup of coffee.

"It sure was. Is she still asleep?" He ends his question with a smirk.

"Yup. I thought she'd stay down for the count after the first blackout, but the girl has stamina. I think it may have been the sex swing that took the rest of her energy."

"No way. It was the three orgasms we gave her on that swing," he mutters, before taking a sip of coffee.

"Yeah. Can I keep it, or are you taking it home?"

Cooper shakes his head as he takes a seat on the stool next to me. "All yours, man." His face turns serious when he tells me, "I think we should tell her. This morning in fact. I want her to know."

I raise my brow. "Everything? Are you sure?"

He's quiet for a beat as if working things out in his head. "Yes." His response is hesitant and filled with worry.

"It's better if we give her a partial truth. Sometimes you have to tell a woman bad news in doses. It lessens the blow. Maybe keep my part in this out. Danni was doing me a favor getting her to join the agency, and she really doesn't need to know I own it."

Cooper had been looking for an in with Beth for a couple of months. As soon as he'd seen her on the street, all of his feelings for her came back with a vengeance. We looked into her and found out where she worked and who her friends were. Apparently, I'd fucked a few or ten of them, including Danni. She knew of me, but not who I was. We didn't run in the same circles back then. I might have only spoken to her that one time, but I gave her a fake name.

It was just a matter of getting her to join and take the leap. I had my IT guy do a little computer manipulation, and like magic, we ended up being the best choices.

"Yeah, you're right. I don't think she'd take kindly to you owning the company, or for that matter, using her friend."

"Please," I retort. "Danni would never allow herself to be used unless it felt good. I gave her a carte blanche membership as payment. The last I heard, she threw a fetish party for herself, three other men, and another woman."

Cooper laughs. "And how is it that you have never been arrested?"

"Simple. I'm smart."

"Smart-ass."

"Fuck you, Josh." His former name slips out. I haven't used it in years, so it sounds foreign on my tongue. "She seems happy. Maybe wait another day to—"

A clearing of a throat startles Cooper and me.

Shit, Beth.

Based on her facial expression, I know that she heard at least a portion of our conversation. She's wearing Cooper's oversized sweatpants and a T-shirt with flip-flops. We didn't even hear her move about in the other room. Cooper goes to approach her, but she halts him.

"Anything to get laid huh, Josh?" Her fists clench at his side and then she turns to me. "I guess you got another notch on your belt. So glad I could be of service."

Her face is red, and the timbre in her voice venomous as she lays on one final blow to Cooper. "You know what Coo— I mean Josh. I was considering starting something with you. I thought you were funny and kind, but it was all a lie, right? You're just like the rest of the men in this world. Only good for a quick fuck. If I need you again, let me know if you're going rate changes, yeah?"

At that parting jab, she storms out the door, Cooper charging after her.

CHAPTER 8

Then: Fourteen Years ago

COOPER/JOSHUA

"JOSH," Jared waved his hand in front of my face, "are you even paying attention to me?"

Of course, I wasn't. I was staring at the girl sitting at the top of the pyramid. I'd had a crush; no, I'd been in love with her since I'd stepped into the school junior year. She didn't even know I existed.

The popular sophomore cheerleader with the shiny red hair and pale blue eyes was all that I'd thought about these days. The only chance I'd gotten to see her was during a mutual study hall, and there, during her daily practice. I always hid under the bleachers with my friend, Jared. We'd smoked to pass the time. He thought I was insane for wanting the girl so much, but I couldn't help myself.

"Earth to Josh." Jared shook my shoulder.

"What," I snapped, finally focusing my attention on him.

"I asked if you plan on asking ginger over there to the dance."

Shoving my hands in my pocket, I shrugged. "I don't know, maybe."

Jared rolled his eyes. "Seriously, man, act like you're older than her and grow some balls. She's not that intimidating."

But she really was, I'd thought to myself. Bethany Phillips was beautiful, and I'd been a scrawny, big nosed, blond-haired loser. "She'd probably say no if I asked her anyway."

"I can't believe that you're forcing me to say this." Jared ran his fingers through his hair. "You are a good-looking guy, and she'd be a fool not to be interested. There, I said it. You're such a tool sometimes; do you know that?"

"A tool that saved your life."

Jared's face cringed at the reminder, not because I'd saved his life, but for what caused him to almost die.

Friends since the age of seven, Jared had always been the type of guy who'd try anything. About a year ago, he'd had the bright idea to trip on mushrooms. I'd declined at first but then figured what could go wrong.

For us, everything did.

Our town had a series of rock formations, some at least thirty feet off the ground. In our tripped-out state, we'd decided it would be a cool idea to follow the trail through the woods and take photos from the top of one of the mini mountains. At some point, Jared slipped and fell over the cliff. Before I'd looked over the edge, I'd assumed he died. I was relieved that his hand caught a protruding tree branch instead. I'd hoisted him up with monumental effort, but it hadn't been easy. After everything was said and done, he'd told me how grateful he was that I'd saved his life, and that one day he'd do something awesome for me. I'd hoped so. Maybe he could get Beth to like me. I'd chuckled at the thought. Never in a million years would Beth be the least bit interested in me.

"I need to head home," Jared announced as he bent over to grab his backpack.

I gave him a questioning look and he grinned in response.

"The cheerleader next to your girl is meeting me there."

"You have to tell me one day how you get so much tail."

Shrugging, Jared told me, "I know what they want, sexually, and word of my awesomeness with the lady population has already spread throughout the entire school."

I shook my head. "You know, normal high school teenagers date one girl."

"Who says I'm normal?" He laughed. "I bet you'd change your tune if you were in the same position."

"Nah. I only want one girl." I chanced a glance over at Beth again who was packing up her stuff. I realized I'd stared a little too long when I heard Jared groan from beside me.

"One day you'll get some balls, my friend." Jared punched me in the shoulder.

"Perhaps," I mumbled.

"Oh shit. I have the perfect idea."

"I know all about your ideas." I rolled my eyes. "Usually they involve one or both of us getting hurt, in trouble with our parents, or both. What category does this fall into?"

"Shut up. It's foolproof, but don't be weird about it."

"Fine. Tell me your master plan."

"Okay." He rubbed his hands together like a mad scientist planning world domination. "We've already established that you like Beth, but you have no game."

"Thanks for the vote of confidence," I muttered, crossing my arms over my chest.

"Well, it's true." Jared gave me a pointed look. "Anyway, what if I showed you the ropes, you know, how to do things and such."

My brows furrowed. "Things like what?"

"How to talk to girls, and umm ... what to do with them."

I opened my mouth to speak; however, Jared interrupted me.

"Listen, I know you're a virgin, and it's no big deal. I figure you need some guidance." I must have looked freaked out or worried because he continued. "Relax. I'm not going to confess that I'm in love with you, and want to do you or something. I only want to help you because I owe you my life and this is how I want to repay you. Hell, maybe I can make money on this one day. Before you tell me no, think about."

Letting out a long sigh, I nodded at him as he left. I'd always admired Jared because he couldn't give two shits what people thought of him. He never fit into any of the typical high school student roles. Not only was he smart and driven but he'd always marched to his own tune, which would make him successful in the future.

Grabbing my backpack, I walked around the bleachers in the direction of my house, which happened to be where Beth was packing up the remainder of her stuff. I kept my head down as I passed her, but paused when she spoke.

"Josh, right?"

At her using my name, my heart pounded so fast I thought it would come out of my chest. I kept imagining the movie *Alien,* where the creature ate his way out of the man's stomach. I prayed it wouldn't happen to me. That would be really embarrassing.

Turning around, I stared at her, saying nothing. I was too mesmerized by the smile she beamed at me. I was fairly certain she was asking me something, but the way she said my name was on repeat in my brain. She brought me out of my fever state when she touched my shoulder and shook me, the warmth of her hand awakening the senses in my body, including my unused dick.

"You in there, Josh?" She was still grinning.

"Yeah … Umm, what did you say?" The question came out in a mumble, and I was surprised she understood me.

"Well, first I said your name, and then I asked if you could come to my house later."

My eyes went as wide as saucers at the invite. I had no idea why she would want me in her house. Thoughts of Jared's offer ran through my head. I should take him up on it because I had no fucking clue what to do.

"Your house?"

"Yes. Your friend Carl, with the dark hair, overheard me complaining about Mr. McCoy's math class, and said that you tutor sophomores. Can you help me?"

I wanted to laugh because I had no friend named Carl, and I'd never taken Mr. McCoy's class. The setup reeked of Jared, but I couldn't be mad at him. He just wanted me happy.

Before I had the chance to agree, an extremely large lacrosse player stalked in our direction. When he arrived, he immediately put his arm around Beth, giving me, a scowling look the entire time.

"Hey, Lou," she said as he gave her a kiss on the cheek. It wasn't a boyfriend type of peck. I classified it as brotherly. Lou however, did not remove his arm.

"Is this loser bothering you?"

Beth tapped his appendage, obviously in an attempt to soothe the beast.

"Calm down. I was asking Josh to tutor me is all."

"Not gonna happen," the man-beast replied sharply. "I talked to Quincy's sister and she said she would. That way we can study together."

Beth turned to me, her expression apologetic. "Guess I don't need you anymore." What she said felt like a thousand knives stabbing me inside my chest. I knew she didn't mean to injure me, but it did. It was then I realized how much I really wanted her.

"Okay," I muttered as I walked away. At that

moment, I swore to myself that I would do whatever it took to have her, even if it meant crossing certain lines.

CHAPTER 9

Romance Is Dead

COOPER/JOSHUA

"BETH," I shout as she runs down the hall to the elevators. "Wait, just let me explain."

Pausing, she whirls around to face me, her eyes filled with anger and ... hurt.

"Explain?" Her voice is quiet, but I'm sure she's pissed. "Explain what exactly? How you manipulated me into sleeping with you? Or how you lied about who you were? I can't decide which one I want to hear first from you, *Joshua*. By the way, the new nose and hair are a nice touch, but it's your eyes that give you away."

She turns to the elevator and presses the down button, but I grab her arm and turn her to me again. "I'm not finished with you yet."

Despite her struggle, I pull her into a kiss. Though she fights me at first, her resolve eventually dissipates. In no way do I see this as a sign that she forgives me. In fact, I'm proven correct when she knees me in the balls, forcing me to let her go and hold myself.

"Fuck you, Josh," she growls, actually growls, as the elevator arrives. "Don't ever call me again," she says as she enters. "And tell the other liar to stay away from me too."

A lump forms in my throat as the doors close. I can't believe that she found out this way. I knew I should have said something sooner. It seemed like a great plan at first, but now …

"Give her some time," Jared says from behind me, placing a hand on my shoulder. "She can't stay mad forever, and when you explain to her about your endless pining crap, she'll let you back in."

"Would you?" I ask him, turning around.

"I'm not the person to ask. I've never had a relationship, but I can read people. She likes you, that I'm sure of. She's probably trying to reconcile the new and old you. Give her tonight, and then grovel tomorrow."

He hands me my T-shirt, shoes, and jacket. "Go home, I'll clean up here."

I smile wryly. "Thanks."

About thirty minutes later, I arrive home. I want to call her so bad, but Jared says to give her time. Scotch seems like a good way to deal with the waiting, so I indulge. One glass becomes four or five.

I'm drunk, and it's because of this fact I do something idiotic—like text Beth.

Me: I love you. I always have.

Dread runs through me as I stare at the phone, waiting for a response I don't expect to come. Until it does.

Beth: You barely know me.

I smile at her response because she has no idea how much I do.

Me: I know you bite your bottom lip when you're nervous, that you twirl your hair with your fingers when thinking. You smile at everyone, no matter if you like them or not. You look hot in a skirt.

Beth: You lied to me.

**Me: I know, and I'm sorry. I want to see you.
To explain.**

It kills me that she doesn't respond, but I under-stand. What could I really say to her? I'm currently drunk and it would probably come out all wrong.

**Me: Meet me tomorrow at the coffee shop
where we first met. Please.**

Beth: I'm not sure I can.

**Me: Sure, you can. Tell you what; I'll be there
at 1:00 p.m. If you don't show up, then I'll
take it as you ending us. I'll never bother you
again.**

How I'm going to be able to stay away from her is anyone's guess, but I'll tell her anything she needs to hear if the endgame brings her back to me.

Beth: I'll think about it. Good night, Josh.

**Me: Cooper. Haven't gone by Josh since I was
a teen.**

Beth: I like Josh. Goodbye.

Tossing my phone on the couch next to me, I stand. I'm a bit unsteady on my feet, but I manage to make it to the bathroom, take a shower and get into bed without killing myself.

As I lie under my duvet, I think about all the things I'll say to her tomorrow. I'm also hoping and praying what Jared said is true. She'll forgive me. Because without her, I'm nothing.

CHAPTER 10

That's What Friends Are For

BETHANY

How DID I not know it was him?

The question has been rattling around in my head since I left the hotel this morning. I knew there was something about him, but with that new face, I didn't put two and two together.

Joshua.

I never knew his last name and had only spoken to him once. I do recall catching him staring at me a couple of times during study hall, but I was too immature to do anything about it. I was more concerned with being the perfect student, the perfect daughter, and the perfect cheerleader, that I missed out. I remember. He had the sweetest smile. One that really hasn't changed, the more I think about it.

Drowning my sorrows in red wine on Christmas of all days, I decided to call Carrie and confess everything. She was pissed about me keeping the dating agency secret, but what upset her most is that I didn't invite her to join. If Jared wasn't such a lying asshole, then maybe I would try to get her in. She told me that she'd be here in twenty minutes to quote "punch me in the boob" as punishment. I gladly agreed because being alone on the holiday would have been another stab to the gut.

While I wait for Carrie's arrival, I make the proverbial call to the parents. They're usually vacationing somewhere tropical during Christmas. They are not big fans of the cold, and I don't blame them. Maybe I should have spent my money on a trip to Cabo instead. Sunburn pain heals a lot easier than emotional pain.

Fucking Coop ... Joshua.

The door buzzer alerts me to an arrival. Carrie has her own key, so like a true Brooklyn resident, I'm suspicious of any unknown guest.

"Can I help you?" I push the intercom and question whoever it is.

"Let me up. It's Jared. Please."

"Screw you." I snap.

"Come on, Beth. Give me five minutes."

I release the button to ignore him, but he continues with the incessant ringing.

"What," I snarl, irritated with this asshole.

"I'm going to keep ringing your door until you let me up, so get used to the sound."

The fucker pushes the button in the melody of "Deck the Halls." I only know this because I can hear him sing through the intercom in conjunction with the bell.

"Fine." I buzz him in before he disturbs my sweet neighbor and her brother. They tend to stay secluded during the Christmas since they lost their parents, and Jared isn't the kind of company they need to be disturbed by.

While I wait for the idiot, I count to one hundred. It's the only way to calm myself. He knocks on the door, and I open it, blocking his path.

"Hey." Jared gives me a wry smile.

"Hi."

"Fancy meeting you here?"

Frowning, I point out, "You came to my apartment."

"Oh yeah." He runs a hand across his forehead, wiping away a barely-there sheen of sweat. His eyes dart from side to side as if he's following one of the bouncy balls that dance over words in a sing-along video.

"So, can I come in, or are you going to make me stand in the doorway and grovel."

"This is rich. Mr. Bossman wants to apologize to me?"

"If you let me in, I will explain."

Glaring at him for a beat, I contemplate punching him in the stomach and slamming the door in his face. I don't like manipulators, especially hot ones such as this dick. Though it would be nice to know why they played me. Even if his presence makes me want to hit something, I'll tolerate him for now.

Walking into the room, he goes right into it telling me, "Coop is like foil, flat and boring."

"Hold on a second," I interrupt. "What's this about foil?"

He shakes his head. "Umm ... Never mind. I'm just saying that you need to give Coop another chance. He's wanted you for-fucking-ever, and if I have to hear any more about how beautiful, kind, and sexy you are, then I might murder him."

I cross my arms in front of my chest. "If that's your way of explaining and apologizing, then you're wasting my time." I point toward the door. "The exit is that way."

As I turn to walk away, Jared grabs me by the arm and turns me to face him.

"Explanation, right." He lets out a sigh, and begins, "Coop … I mean Josh and I became friends at a young age through our parents. We constantly hung out, and he was always the shy one. He never dated or mentioned a girl until he went to our high school and saw you. You were all he talked about. I wanted to make him happy because the man saved my life. There was a cliff and well, it doesn't matter. I owed him one, and I thought the best way to do it was through you."

Well, I wasn't expecting him to lay that on me. Perhaps he's not as much of a self-centered asshole as I assumed; which I guess is a good thing. Biting my bottom lip, I offer him a seat. He slides in the spot next to me and continues on.

"Coop would kill me if he knew I was telling you this, but, that day you blew him off, he agreed to let me teach him how to handle women. However, right before we had the chance to start, he got into that terrible accident. By the time senior year came around, he was recovering and getting used to the new him. When we finally began our training, the goal was to, of course, teach him the ropes, making him into someone else. He was the one who decided to legally change his name to Cooper. Eventually, becoming the man you know today. Instead of going after you like he planned, he met his ex-wife, and well you know how that turned out."

This new information has me feeling sorry for

him. He went through so much … for me. His lie wasn't bad; it was more of an omission. Jared was the one who manipulated me, so technically, he's at fault.

"When he saw you again months ago, it was like high school all over again. I had to find an in for him, and Danni was it. Sorry about that by the way."

I give Jared a reluctant smile because I can tell he's being sincere. If Carrie wanted me to do something as crazy as this, then I probably would.

"It was a shit thing to do, and as an adult, I should have forced Cooper to approach you." He grins. "I'm not sorry about last night, though. My dick still remembers that pussy of yours."

Rolling my eyes, I inform him, "I've had better."

"Liar," he retorts. If I recall, you passed out twice, and let's not forget the 'fuck me harder' demands you made. I counted seventeen."

"Now I see why Cooper tells you to fuck off. You're annoying."

"What can I say? It's a gift. All joking aside, I think you should give him another chance. I'm not saying that you should go to him now because you and I both know that he's probably drunk. Maybe give it a day, and then work it out."

"What makes you so sure that I'll give him the time of day ever again?"

"Please. I can read people like a book and you, my

dear, are on the verge of caving. If blaming me pushes you over the edge, then have at it, yeah."

I open my mouth to speak, but nothing comes out. Carrie chooses this moment to arrive, using her spare key to enter. She catches sight of Jared and lays into him immediately.

"What the hell is asshole number two doing here?" She scans the room. "Is asshole number one here too? I'm feeling the need to punch someone in the dick." She glares at Jared. He covers his crotch at her threat.

"Calm down, Carrie." I go over to her, holding her in place. "We've worked it out."

"In twenty minutes? Is his cock so magical that it brainwashed you into thinking his actions were okay?

"What is this fascination she has with the male anatomy?" Jared murmurs, continuing to keep his hands in place.

"Zip it, Carrington." I scowl at him and then inform Carrie, "It's fine, babe. Jared and I have an understanding, so no penis punching, m'kay?"

Jared hesitantly removes his hands and stands, skirting his way around Carrie and me.

"Don't forget what I told you, Beth, and trust me. He's worth it." With that last declaration, Jared steps out of the apartment.

"You sure it's all good?"

"Yes." I nod, smiling. "But since you're here, let's finish this bottle of wine, listen to holiday music, and

I'll give you the full details of how those two rocked my world."

"Goodie." She rubs her hands together like a mad scientist. "I've been dying to know if porn is an accurate depiction of what happens in the real world."

"It is." I grin as I explain why I'll be buying her the Womanizer Deluxe as a belated Christmas present.

Later that night, Cooper sends some interesting texts. A couple are shocking, but after speaking with Jared, I'd expect nothing less from him. I forgive him, for the most part, but as a tiny payback, I might make him sweat a little.

CHAPTER 11

Hearts and Flowers

COOPER/JOSHUA

I'M on my third cup of coffee and my nerves are shot. I'm surprised I haven't run to the bathroom like a preschooler, but I'm afraid I'll miss her entrance ... if she's coming. The woman can really make one, that's for sure. I'd watch her enter study hall, and I swear it was in slow motion, just like the movies. He red hair would bounce and everything.

"God, I'm such a tool," I mutter, rubbing my hand over my face. After checking my watch for the millionth time, I confirm that she's thirty minutes late. Fear sets in as I come to the realization that she's not coming, and why would she? I'm a lying asshole. Who would want anything to do with me?

Just as I prepare to stand, resigning myself to a life without her in it, a warm hand touches my shoulder, and I know it's her. I'd felt this type of sensation years ago, back when I was geeky Josh. As confident Cooper, it feels exactly the same.

"Where are you going, Josh?" she whispers from behind me, her soothing voice causing me to relax in my seat.

"Was waiting for you," I mumble. I grasp her hand, tugging her around so I can see her. "And you're late."

"Nope. I've been here, watching you since you arrived."

"How?"

She places a finger over my lips to silence me. "I can stalk a little too."

I give a playful nip at her finger before she pulls her hand away. She doesn't seem mad, but I need to see where we are before I get comfortable. I motion for her to take a seat, and then I begin to speak. I explain to her about my high school crush, my college detour into married life, and how I found her again. She doesn't appear surprised at the last part, which confuses me.

"I should have told you sooner, but I was afraid something like this would happen."

"Jared told me everything," she confesses, biting her lip. "I wasn't going to see him at first, but he's a persistent man."

"Yup," I acknowledge.

"I'm not saying that what you did was okay, and I don't forgive you, completely," she adds. "But I think there's something here. Love, lust, or whatever you want to call it. Our night together was an eye-opening experience for me, and I'd like to do it again."

My eyes drop to the table in disappointment. I don't want to share her again, even with Jared.

"Josh," she calls, and I look up. "With only you. That thing with Jared was a one-timer. To be honest, I can only handle one of you. If you want to in the future, I'd be willing, but right now, no."

I feel like a kid on Christmas morning. I want to push her against the wall and kiss her, but it wouldn't be appropriate. Instead, I lean forward, giving her a gentle press of my lips. I slip my tongue in partially, doing a quick sweep, just to taste the inside.

After breaking our kiss, I tell her, "I love you, even if you don't feel the same. Though I should tell you that you eventually will. Cooper can be very persuasive." I waggle my eyebrows.

"Calm down there, stallion," she quips. "I'd like to

get to know Josh first. Cooper can show up in the bedroom if you want. Can you arrange that?"

My lips twitch. "Yes, I can."

"I should tell you. My friend Carrie suggested that I punch you in the dick, but I told her that I kneed you in the balls already. She wants to meet you."

Chuckling I say, "As long as she doesn't come anywhere near my dick or balls, then fine. They belong solely to you now."

EPILOGUE

One Year Later

*J*ARED

BLUE BALLS HAVE BECOME an integral part of my life. I haven't had sex in over three months. I tried, but it's as if my dick has suddenly gotten a conscience. I keep occupied with other things, such as spending time with Cooper. Beth hangs with us on occasion.

Their wedding was fun. It was a small ceremony in Prospect Park, which consisted of twenty-five guests, and their new puppy, Scruffy, for a ring bearer.

It was also the last time I got laid.

I blame that viper with the sleek dark brown hair, which I immensely enjoyed pulling as I fucked her. After looking into her silver-gray eyes glittering in the moonlight, I knew I was in trouble. I call her Voldemort because she's an evil soul stealer and shouldn't ever be named. Good pussy has never crippled me before. I always come out on top.

Until now.

New Year's is about making resolutions, and unlike some, I plan on keeping mine. I won't let that she-devil keep me out of commission any longer. I will have sex again, if it's the last thing I do.

-THE END-

Thank you for reading. If you loved Cooper & Beth's story, please consider leaving a spoiler-free review on the site you purchased the book from.

FINISHING THE NEW YEAR

For a sample of Finishing in the New Year, Jared & Marla's and book, keep reading.

PROLOGUE

RESOLUTION: DECEMBER 31ST

JARED

EMPTY PUSSY.

Cooper told me about this phenomenon once and I didn't believe him until today. In fact, I'm staring at one passed out in my bed. I have a lot of respect for women who know what they want sexually and go after it; I actually prefer fucking those types. As of this moment my priorities have shifted and it only took a night of extreme sex with his woman, Beth, and Cooper as a third. That shit was intense, life altering, and damn mind-blowing.

Let me be clear. This isn't a team Cooper or team Jared situation, meaning I'm not upset she didn't choose me. Rather I'd like to find a woman to worship as much as Cooper does Beth. I'm a determined motherfucker and being as such, I make a promise to myself. As the clock ticks down to midnight, I smile, knowing for damn sure I'll make it come true.

CHAPTER 1

CHAPTER 1

THE ORIGIN OF BLUE BALLS: seven months later

JARED

"ARE you sure you want to do this?" I ask my friend Josh, as I lean back in the comfortable leather armchair.

"Duh ... Yes," he declares confidently, adjusting his tie. "I am wearing a fancy Michael Kors suit, and in case you haven't noticed, we're in Baldwin's Formal Wear Shop." He motions to the surrounding room filled with a variety of tuxedos, ties, and other men's wedding accessories.

Josh, yes, Cooper legally changed his name back, is getting hitched to Beth. It only took a month for her to confess her love to him, and two for the woman to agree to marriage. Don't get me wrong, I'm happy for the guy, but I think this relationship might be going a little fast. They were separated for years, and people change, right?

"I see," I mumble, taking a sip of my complimentary champagne. My eyes catch sight of his narrowed ones in the mirror and he turns to face me, his expression guarded.

"What the hell is wrong with you, Jared?" He folds his arms across his chest. "You were the one who convinced her to see me again. I thought you'd be happy about this."

"I am. It's just …" I pause, attempting to organize my thoughts. Who am I kidding? I'm damn elated for him. Though slightly embarrassing, I confess the true reason behind my un-Jared like attitude. "I might be jealous of you two."

"The great Jared Carrington jealous of a loser like me?" He smirks. "Stop the presses."

"Fuck you."

"Well, perhaps if you didn't sleep with the entire population of Manhattan, then you would meet a nice girl to settle down with."

"That's the thing. I'm jealous of what you have and I'm not completely sure I want to settle down. I like having the freedom to do whoever I want." Total bullshit. I could go the monogamy route if it's with the right woman.

Josh shakes his head at me. "You realize that's crazy. You can't have your cake and eat it too."

"I didn't say anything about cake. I want an open relationship is all."

"Good luck finding a woman to agree to that. I've only seen it happen on reality television. You're better off becoming a polygamist and moving to a place where it's prominent. I believe it's legal in the middle of the country. They have cheap housing if you're game."

"And move out of New York?" I scoff, taking a final swig of my drink. "No one does that, ever."

"How about you use that agency of yours to find a woman? There are plenty to choose from who won't mind if you dipped your dick in other places."

"Nah. I don't shit where I work."

"But you did fuck Danni."

"Yes," I begrudgingly agree, reminiscing about that wild night with the blonde temptress. She's the first woman I ever let tie me up, and by let, I mean she distracted me with her dick sucking skills so that she could cuff me to her bed. I was not a fan. "I slept with her before she joined my agency. Therefore it doesn't count. Besides, she's a handful, and definitely off limits."

"I get that." He turns to face the mirror, studying his reflection. "But you have to figure out what you want. I have my happily ever after, and I'd like you to get yours too."

"Slow down, Oliver." A female voice with a sexy as fuck rasp shouts at what appears to be a teenager barreling toward us, bringing my senses to attention. Meticulously scanning the room, I'm unable to pinpoint the direction the sound came from. "I said, stop." Frustration is my first name, as I still can't find the elusive woman having this effect on me, therefore I focus on the kid who abruptly skids to a halt. The daredevil was mere inches from running into another tailor carrying fresh glasses of champagne for the groomsmen a few rooms over. Josh strides past me, greeting the kid with a hug, doing a quick muss of his hair. A returning smile is exchanged, Josh ending the hello with a pat on the teen's back.

Feeling left out, I walk over to introduce myself, but my ability to speak the English language evaporates as soon as the woman in question comes into view. She says something that involves words, however I'm so enamored by her beauty I don't hear it. Instead my gaze travels the length of her, taking in every sexy inch of attractiveness.

The olive tone of her skin complements her long

chocolate brown hair, its silky texture I would kill to run my fingers through. She's got gorgeous curves and long legs to match, the smoothness of her skin evident due to the clingy miniskirt covering her shapely ass. I try not to stare at her tits, but the lacey white tank top makes it difficult to ignore them. I'm a man who appreciates a beautiful body and she has it all, her outfit alone is giving me a hard-on. When I finally meet her eyes, I fight the urge to take a step back, the silvery-gray hue of them jarring. Their unique color has a boldness about them and at the same time shine with honesty and warmth, her heart-shaped face adding to the allure.

She gives me a once-over, her eyes flashing with possible interest or could it be annoyance? Whatever is going on in that pretty little head of hers, I have every confidence I'll attract her. I am the shit after all.

This is the first time in my life I've ever craved a connection with a woman, and I'm claiming this vision standing in front of me.

"Hello, Jared?" Josh breaks me out of my trance. "Did you hear what I said?"

"He looks confused," the sexy vixen tells Josh. "Should we call an ambulance? These suit types always have some kind of ADHD or anxiety issues."

Josh's laughter finally gets me to say something.

"I'm Jared, and you are?" I give her one of my

classic smolders. It works one hundred percent of the time, and this should be no different.

"He looks constipated," Oliver blurts out.

I turn to him and glare, hoping he gets my shut the fuck up vibe, but he returns with a sly smile. Josh catches the exchange of looks between us and shakes his head.

"Marla, this is my very strange friend, Jared. Jared, Marla." He then points to the kid. "The smirking teenager is her brother, Oliver."

I extend my hand to shake hers, but am blocked by the teenage asshole, who grabs my hand instead.

"Oliver Rivera, nice to meet you." He applies pressure to my palm like this is some sort of power play. I inwardly laugh because the little twerp is no match for me. In retaliation, I grip his harder to prove a point. Don't fuck with me.

"Ouch," he yelps, jerking his hand back. A self-satisfying smile spreads across my face, though it doesn't last. In the next moment I detect a sharp throbbing pain on my temple, the palm of Marla's hand being the culprit of my injury.

"What's wrong with you, Jerry? He's just a teenager." She pulls that fucker in her arms and hugs him. He gives me a look that says fuck off. Of course neither Josh nor Marla see this.

Josh mouths, "what the fuck to me" and I shrug noncommittally.

"Well, Jerry. Are you going to apologize?"

"Sorry, Marla. I forget how strong I am. And my name is—"

"Don't apologize to me." She points to Oliver, who is now staring at me with his arms crossed. "You injured his hand."

Narrowing my eyes at the boy I reluctantly mumble, "Sorry." The corner of his mouth curves and I want to punch him. Oliver eventually nods in acceptance, his eyes filled with mirth.

Bastard.

Fuck. This isn't going well. I need suave master of the universe Jared to make an appearance. Not the bumbling idiot Jerry. First impressions matter and I always excel at them. I'm not sure how this interaction went off the rails and I have to get it back on track.

Sensing my panic, Josh throws me a bone, changing the subject. "How's the internship going?"

"Awesome," Oliver replies, his attention now focused on Josh. "Beth said they might hire me part-time if I keep up the good work. Plus with her in my corner I got this one in the bag."

"He definitely does," Marla finally speaks, giving her brother a friendly shove. "Oliver is the smart one in our family."

"I was top of my class at the University of Pennsylvania." Immediately after the sporadic declaration passes my lips I know I fucked-up. My skin pales as three heads slowly turn in my direction, each expression different. Josh's eyes are lit with humor while the woman of my dreams scowls, her brother glaring daggers at me.

"I'm not at your level, Jerry, but I will be one day. I have a hard time getting top notch grades with my dyslexia, but my teachers are helping me out."

And now I feel like a piece of shit.

"Uh …" Josh says absolutely nothing to save me from my embarrassment. I've only ever seen him speechless when it's Beth related, though there's a first time for everything as I'm learning at the present.

"Anyway." Marla drags out the word. "Oliver has his suit and we'll see you at the wedding if not before." She gives me a final perusal, turns on her heels, and walks away. I glance in her direction, hoping to get a full view of her ass, but her brother senses my intention giving me the finger. Once again, Josh doesn't see the acts of the duplicitous teenager, too busy staring at me, his expression befuddled.

"What just happened here?"

"Not important," I cut him off. "What you should be divulging is the telephone number of the fine piece of ass that just sauntered out."

"Nuh uh. I'm not your pimp and Marla is off limits. This means, one less notch on your bedpost. Besides, I think she hates you."

"No way. She smiled at me." Actually it was more like a grimace.

"Were you paying attention just now? You gawked at her like a stalker, you tried to break her teenaged brother's hand, and you called said brother, with dyslexia I might add, an idiot. Do I have all that right so far?" He's right, but I'm not one to give up when I want something this much.

"I've never seen you like this before. You were a blundering clown and it was entertaining." He laughs. "I can't wait to tell Beth. You are not going to live this one down, buddy."

"If you spill I will end you," I snap, my fists clenching at my sides. I am in no way pissed at my friend, more upset with myself. I'm good-looking and confident as hell, therefore I should be able to handle a short interaction with a woman. She makes me stupid. Perhaps it's best I end the pursuit before it begins, continuing to claim easy pussy. Even as the thought crosses my mind I remind myself of the course I chose at the beginning of the year. Easy equals empty and I damn sure don't want that.

"Calm down, Jared. I don't get why you're so—" He pauses mid-sentence, as if putting it all together. "Wait. This isn't part of your quest to find a perfect woman? If so, then I'm definitely not giving you her number. I don't want her to be a practice run for your crazy. She's been through enough already."

I've never considered committing a violent crime, but Josh is slowly causing me to change my mind. "A friend isn't supposed to withhold information from another and I believe you owe me one for your current relationship status," I inform him.

"True, but my fiancée is close friends with Marla, and I don't want to do anything to jeopardize that. Unfortunately, you are on the shit list. I mean she calls you Jerry."

"Not my fault and the name issue is a minor fix," I retort. "At least get her to meet me so that I can apologize for being an asshole."

"I'm not sure that's a good idea. You seem to have foot and mouth disease with her." Josh rubs his chin. "But, it's fun watching you sweat." He sighs. "Fine. Marla comes to Beth's office on Tuesdays to bring Oliver lunch around noon. If you happen to drop by, then you may run into her."

I almost kiss him on the cheek for the intel, but I'm a man, and we give nods and chin lifts. "Thanks."

"Don't get me in trouble with Beth, or it will be me that ends you."

"When have I ever done that?"

"Fuck off, Jared."

GRAB YOURS!

Grab your copy of Finishing in the New Year on Amazon today!

getbook.at/FITNY

ACKNOWLEDGMENTS

Thank you once again to my husband who supports me 110%. I don't know what I would do without him.

Thanks to my partner in crime, Amy, you do so much for me. I'd be lost in the internet abyss if you weren't here.

Klaire, you are the best. You make everything I write so much better.

Lauren, for being another set of eyes, and listening to my crazy.

Virginia, thanks for putting it all together for me!

Danni S., Mel T., Nichole W., and Shannon S., thank you for letting me use your names for characters. I promise, I didn't picture your face at all when I wrote those scenes.

My street team Robin, Lynn, and Mayra. Thank

you for taking time out during the day to share for me. Your help is much appreciated.

Thank you most of all to the readers. Without you, I wouldn't be able to live out my dream.

WHERE TO FIND THE AUTHOR

Where to find the author:
FB Group => http://bit.ly/FBKittyDen
Amazon Page => http://bit.ly/KrystynaAllyn
Newsletter => http://bit.ly/2MYUI5t
Website => https://www.krystynaallyn.com/

ABOUT THE AUTHOR

Krystyna lives in somewhere USA with her amazingly awesome husband. Though she works full time, blogs, and reads like a maniac, she still manages to find the time to write all her crazy stories.

Her hobbies include baking, skydiving, karaoke, and general mischief. The list of her favorite authors is endless, so rather than singling out anyone particular, she'll just mention her number one go-to cookie is oatmeal raisin.

Made in the USA
Middletown, DE
27 September 2022

11223706R00086